GUNSMOKE™
BLIZZARD OF LEAD

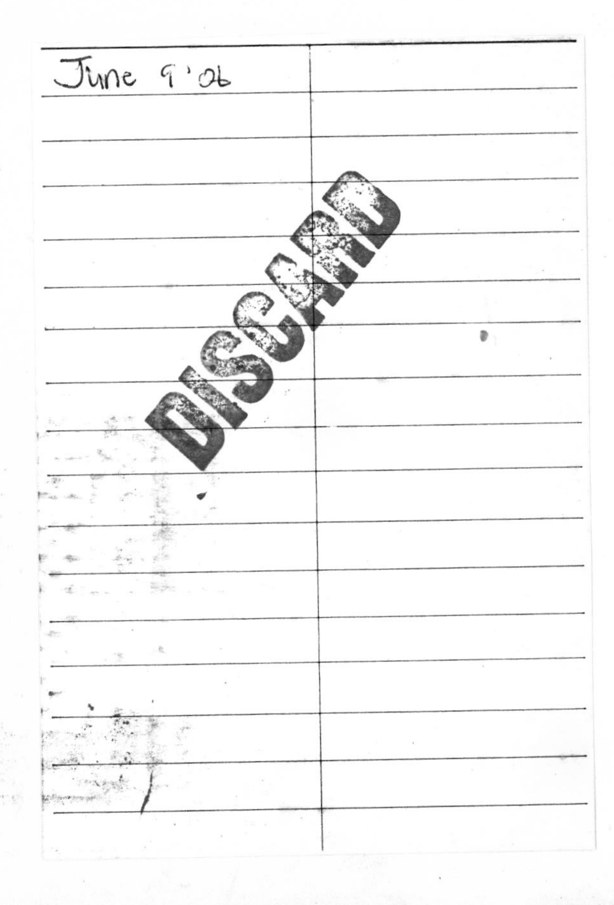

Also by Joseph A. West in Large Print:

Ralph Compton: Blood and Gold
Ralph Compton: Doomsday Rider
Ralph Compton:
Showdown at Two-Bit Creek

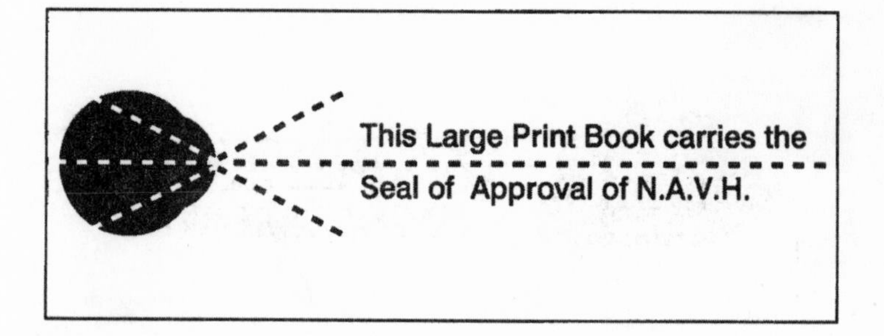

GUNSMOKE™ BLIZZARD OF LEAD

Foreword by James Arness

Joseph A. West

This is a work of fiction. Names, characters, places, and incidents either are the product of the author's imagination or are used fictitiously, and any resemblance to actual persons, living or dead, business establishments, events, or locales is entirely coincidental.

The publisher does not have any control over and does not assume any responsibility for author or third-party Web sites or their content.

Published in 2006 by arrangement with NAL Signet, a division of Penguin Group (USA) Inc.

Wheeler Large Print Western.

The text of this Large Print edition is unabridged.
Other aspects of the book may vary from the original edition.

Set in 16 pt. Plantin by Minnie B. Raven.

Printed in the United States on permanent paper.

Library of Congress Cataloging-in-Publication Data

West, Joseph A.
Gunsmoke : blizzard of lead / by Joseph A. West ; foreword by James Arness.
p. cm. — (Wheeler Publishing large print westerns)
ISBN 1-59722-175-9 (lg. print : sc : alk. paper)
1. Dillon, Matt (Fictitious character) — Fiction. 2. United States marshals — Fiction. 3. Dodge City (Kan.) — Fiction. 4. Large type books. I. Title: Blizzard of lead. II. Title. III. Wheeler large print western series.
PS3573.E8224G86 2006
813′.54—dc22 2005030905

GUNSMOKE™
BLIZZARD OF LEAD

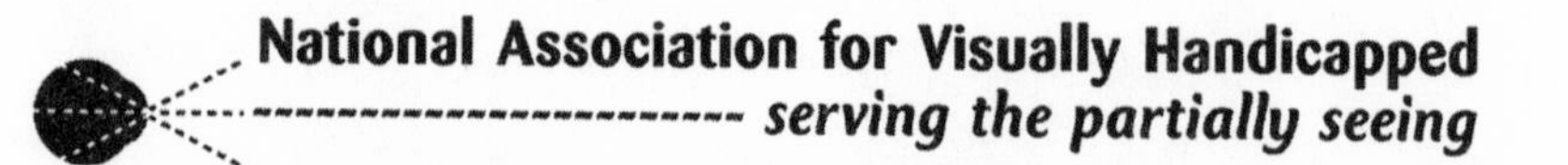

As the Founder/CEO of NAVH, the only national health agency solely devoted to those who, although not totally blind, have an eye disease which could lead to serious visual impairment, I am pleased to recognize Thorndike Press* as one of the leading publishers in the large print field.

Founded in 1954 in San Francisco to prepare large print textbooks for partially seeing children, NAVH became the pioneer and standard setting agency in the preparation of large type.

Today, those publishers who meet our standards carry the prestigious "Seal of Approval" indicating high quality large print. We are delighted that Thorndike Press is one of the publishers whose titles meet these standards. We are also pleased to recognize the significant contribution Thorndike Press is making in this important and growing field.

Lorraine H. Marchi, L.H.D.
Founder/CEO
NAVH

* Thorndike Press encompasses the following imprints: Thorndike, Wheeler, Walker and Large Print Press.

Foreword

As the popularity of *Gunsmoke* grew, we started getting offers to do personal appearances. During the years of *Gunsmoke*, I made many appearances around the country. As we made these appearances, it became apparent that people from all walks of life were fans of the show. *Gunsmoke* meant so many different things to so many people. Even today I receive hundreds of letters telling me how *Gunsmoke* affected the lives of these people. It amazes me how many law enforcement officers we have due to the influence of the show on them. I receive letters from teenagers telling my how much they love the show and watching it with their parents or grandparents. There is one recurring theme in all these letters: *Gunsmoke* stands for value and morality, and the writers all wish we had shows today that were focused on values.

As I wrote my autobiography, I reread many, many letters from fans, which gave me the inspiration to share with everyone stories about my *Gunsmoke* life and my life in general. We decided to do a book signing, and I was overwhelmed at the response and the people who attended. I heard so many times how much *Gunsmoke* meant to everyone. There was one lady who was afraid of flying and had never flown before but did so from Brooklyn in order to be at the signing. Talk about a humbling experience. She was so enthusiastic that she kept all of us energized with her amazing energy and positive outlook. She knew everything about every show and even told us some things we had all forgotten. I told her that she was the ultimate *Gunsmoke* fan. She and a group of ladies — "The Delphi Gang," as we call them — flew in from all over the country for the signing. Most of them had never met one another before that day. They have a Web site forum where they talk about me. I hope it is all good, and they tell me that it is. As a gift, they gave me a bronze cowboy and horse statue, which I will treasure always. It says "Thanks for the Memories" from the Delphi Gang.

Speaking of the book, there was a woman who came to the book signing because we had included a picture of her as a little girl taken at one of my appearances. She is a little older now but she was extremely thrilled to meet me again after all these years.

We had a lot of fun that day because Buck Taylor, Jim Burns, Bruce Boxleitner, Laurie Prange, and a few other actors and stunt men from the show were there. We had an impromptu question-and-answer session with the crowd, which really was fun. The most common question was about my horse, Buck. The answer is that I did have several horses over the years, and every one of them was named Buck. I also can tell you that I don't remember if we ever served real beer but I am sure it happened once in a while. I was asked if we had real beer because someone thought that would account for all the tricks we played on one another, but I can tell you we played tricks day and night for the pure fun of it. They asked if the cast was as close in person as we were on the show, and I can say that we were a close-knit family. During twenty years of shooting, we never had a disagreement, and it was a wonderful show to work on.

I recently received a letter and pictures from a family who have a son with a disability. He loves *Gunsmoke*, and they found that they could teach him things by using his privileges to watch the show as a reward. They even decorated his room to look like the inside of the sheriff's office, including a jail. I am honored and privileged to have been a part of something that is such a positive influence on a young person's life.

Many of you may not be aware that my wife and I support United Cerebral Palsy. We have met the director from Washington, D.C., and are amazed at the work they are doing. The latest development is a clinical trial at UCLA in Los Angeles using a hyperbaric chamber for children with CP. We hope that this makes a difference in the lives of these young children, who have so much to offer our society.

Recently I received another very special presentation from the United States Marshals Service. They presented me with my official retired U.S. marshal's badge. Over the years I have met many of the men and women who have served as marshals; they provide a great service to our country. I was thrilled to be honored by them.

I truly believe in and have lived my life with the same set of values that we portrayed on the show. I also am proud to have served my country in the armed forces and am very proud to be an American. Enjoy this *Gunsmoke* book, and I hope for all of you a healthy and happy life.

— James Arness "Marshal Matt Dillon"

Chapter 1

Blood on the Plains

Winter was cracking down hard on the plains as two riders loped across the frozen prairie north of Dodge City, Kansas, following the tracks of three horsemen.

His face grim and set, Marshal Matt Dillon had already made up his mind. When he caught up with the McCarty brothers he'd give them two choices: surrender or die. They would get no other option.

An upright man doing his best to preserve law and order in a violent, unforgiving land, he judged men by the light of his own experience and inclination because he knew of no other yardstick.

And so he had judged Len, Elam and Jed McCarty and found them wanting — guilty, according to a dozen eyewitnesses, of shooting an unarmed man in the back.

A product of his time and place, Matt Dillon lived by the gunfighter code: a man met his enemies face-to-face, while they were belted and armed and stood ready.

Within the rigid confines of that code, there was little room for cold-blooded murder, and where Western men gathered to talk, no crime was spoken of as lower or more cowardly.

The McCarty boys, tumbleweed trash out of the Neuces Plains country, had killed a gray-haired whiskey drummer for the few dollars in his pockets and the nickel watch, chain and Masonic fob across his belly. Then they had fled Dodge . . . and that was when their options had started to run out.

Now they were fleeing, north across the vast empty plains, perhaps unaware that vengeance rode their back trail and was drawing closer.

"Cold day an' a cold trail, Matthew," Deputy Marshal Festus Haggen said from deep within the upturned collar of his ragged mackinaw. "Neither calc'lated to comfort a man."

Matt turned to his deputy and grinned. "I'm not arguing that the weather's a mite sharp, Festus, but you're wrong about the trail. It isn't cold. Those McCarty boys were less than thirty minutes ahead of us when they hightailed it out of Dodge. They've probably gone a fair piece by now, but not enough." The big marshal's far-seeing eyes scanned the flat, long-riding country ahead of him. "The tracks are headed for Saw Log Creek. I reckon they'll fetch up to the creek, then head east. Plenty of tree cover along the bank to keep them out of sight."

"You figure they know we're after them, Matthew?" Festus asked, his breath smoking like a ten-cent cigar in the frigid air.

The marshal nodded. "They know. And if they don't, they should."

The two riders crossed a small frozen stream running off the bottom reaches of the Saw Log, then headed into a shallow draw between a pair of low humpbacked rises, their crests shaggy with brown-tipped clumps of buffalo grass. A cold wind was blowing steadily from the north and the sky was cloudy, a few stretches of pale blue showing here and there.

Festus, who had been silent for a few minutes, turned to Matt and said: "They say Elam McCarty — that's the oldest brother — has himself a reputation for bein' mighty slick with the Colt. They say he killed a man over in Cheyenne and another down to Texas somewheres. Now I don't know if'n that's true or not, Matthew, but that's what folks say."

"You worried, Festus?" Matt asked, a smile tugging at his lips. "That McCarty feller's reputation nagging at you some?"

"Hell no," the deputy said, suddenly lowered eyebrows revealing his chagrin. "I was just passin' time by makin' polite conversation, is all."

Matt nodded. "Well, if it's any consolation, I heard the same thing my ownself. Seems hard to believe that a backshooting tinhorn like Elam McCarty would have the sand to meet armed men face-to-face and earn himself a gun rep."

"Don't seem right to me either, Matthew," Festus said. "Anyhow, folks have all kinds of queer notions about things and sometimes they say stuff that just ain't true."

"Well, we'll soon find out one way or the other," Matt said.

"That we will," his deputy agreed. Then, more quietly and thoughtfully, he added, "Like you say, one way or t'other."

Around the riders, the vast prairie rolled away flat, featureless and empty in all directions. Even in this year of 1876, settler cabins were still few and far between and only the telegraph poles that marched alongside the tracks of the Santa Fe Railroad broke up the monotony of the landscape. It had snowed an inch or two during the night and a broad white sheet sparkled in the sunlight, reaching into the distance until it met the cloudy bowl of the sky at the horizon.

The land was quiet but for the sighing song of the wind, and it would be months before the crickets once again made their small sounds among the spring grass.

The light was strange, touched with pale amber, and the air was so icy cold, it passed across the tongue like broken glass.

There was an odd tension in Matt Dillon's belly, a coiled spring inside him that had nothing to do with the coming showdown with the McCarty brothers. It came from the land itself. Now and again the wind dropped to a thin whisper, unusual on the plains, as if the silent earth was holding its breath, waiting for something to happen.

Festus felt it too. The deputy gave the sky a wary glance, slowly shook his head, then turned to Matt, his eyes tangled with thought, an unspoken question on his hairy-cheeked face.

"You're feeling it as well, huh?" the marshal asked.

Festus nodded. "Matthew, something jest don't seem right with the day, but I can't seem to set down on a notion about what's wrong."

As his deputy had done earlier, Matt looked up at the sky. "I think there's more snow on the way, Festus. Big snow."

"Sky's clouding over, Matthew, but it don't look like snow clouds to me," Festus said. "Rain maybe?"

"Not rain. I reckon a blizzard is coming," Matt said. "I can feel it, tapping me on the shoulder like a gray ghost."

Festus opened his mouth to speak, but his words died in his throat. He reined in his mule and pointed to the northeast. "Three riders, and it looks like they ain't foggin' it out o' here." The deputy's shocked face revealed his utter disbelief. "Matthew, I reckon it's them McCarty boys — an', hell, they ain't a-runnin'. They're comin' right for us."

Matt's eyes followed his deputy's pointing finger. Moving across the plains from the direction of Saw Log Creek, marked by a straggling line of cottonwoods, men were riding fast toward them, three dark exclamation points of danger against the white backdrop of the snow.

"I thought for sure they'd keep on running," Matt said. His smile tight and grim, he added: "I guess I was wrong."

The big marshal slipped the rawhide thong off the hammer of his Colt, slid the Winchester from the boot under his leg and cranked a round into the chamber. Festus unlimbered his Greener, thumbed open the shotgun and checked the loads. Satisfied, he snapped the scattergun shut and laid it across the saddle horn.

"How do we play this, Matthew?" he asked without turning, his intent eyes fixed on the rapidly approaching horsemen.

"We give them a chance to surrender," Matt said. "After that, if they want to open the ball, then we all choose partners."

Matt and Festus sat their mounts, waiting. Feeling a sudden alertness in his rider, the marshal's big bay got up on his toes, his prancing hooves kicking up brief spurts of snow. Catching the bay's nervousness, Festus' mule tossed her head, her bit jangling, gray Vs of steaming breath jetting from dilated nostrils.

Matt leaned over and patted his horse's neck. "Easy, Buck, easy," he whispered.

The three McCarty brothers came on, spreading out slightly.

"They're ridin' fast," Festus said. "Matthew, you reckon them boys are gonna stop an' palaver like they ought?"

The deputy's question was answered a

heartbeat later. The leading rider threw a rifle to his shoulder and fired. Matt saw the orange muzzle flare and heard a bullet split the air above his head with the spiteful whine of an angry hornet.

"Damn them," he gritted between clenched teeth. "Damn them to hell."

Now only fifty yards separated the two lawmen from the galloping horsemen.

Matt raised his rifle to his shoulder and snapped off a fast shot at a rider breaking to his left. A miss. He levered another round, fired again, and this time the man threw up his arms and tumbled off his horse.

Beside him, the marshal heard the loud *boom! boom!* of Festus' Greener. Torn to shreds by two rounds of double-aught buckshot, a rider slumped in the saddle, swung to his right and fired his rifle from waist level, three shots, very fast. Festus let out a sharp cry and reeled in the saddle, blood suddenly splashing scarlet over the front of his mackinaw. "Matthew," he yelled, "I'm hit hard!"

The third rider, the bearded, long-haired man who had fired the first shot, was charging directly at Matt. Both men fired at the same time and the outlaw jerked upright in the stirrups under the impact of the marshal's .44.40 slug, sagged back into the leather and kicked his mount into a fast gallop. Matt rode to cut the man off. The outlaw's big sorrel was running too fast to stop or swerve and it smashed into Buck. Taken by surprise, the bay lost his footing on the icy snow and went down, falling hard on Matt's left leg. The marshal felt a white-hot bolt of agony from knee to ankle as bone shattered.

Buck scrambled to his feet and staggered into an aimless, unsteady trot. Matt's boot was caught in the stirrup and he bit back an agonized yell as Buck dragged him by his injured leg. After a dozen yards of searing pain, the marshal managed to free his boot and let his leg fall to the ground.

Matt lay stunned for a few moments, his head swimming. He tried to rise, fell back again and stayed still, fighting to stem the nausea churning in his belly.

"Damn you, Dillon. You've killed me," a man snarled from close by. "But I don't plan on going to hell alone. I'm taking you with me."

Matt turned toward the sound of the man's voice and saw the outlaw slowly walking his sorrel toward him, its hooves making a steady *crump, crump* on the hard-frosted snow. Elam McCarty's lips, glistening with blood and saliva, were peeled back from his yellow teeth in a smile, and there was the hungry gleam of the killer wolf in his black eyes.

McCarty raised his rifle at the same instant Matt drew. The marshal was on his back, an awkward position from which to pull a gun, yet his motion was smooth and lightning-fast. His first shot hit McCarty just under the chin, his next, a split second later, crashed into the outlaw's chest.

McCarty's rifle spat flame, but the man was already dead, and his bullet went wild, kicking up a slender spout of snow three feet from where Matt lay.

The marshal thumbed back the hammer of his revolver, but a third shot wasn't needed. Elam McCarty tumbled off his horse and thudded facedown on the frozen ground.

From long habit, Matt shucked the empty shells, reloaded from his cartridge belt and holstered his Colt. Only then did he look around him.

The two other killers lay still, sprawled and undignified in death, the snow under them stained red. Festus was sitting, bent over, rocking slightly, his face ashen. He was trying to keep his pain knotted up inside him. Matt attempted to rise, but the spiking hurt in his broken leg was a vicious living thing that forced him back, groaning, to the ground.

Gritting his teeth, he knew he had to get to his deputy. Festus must be hit hard because he had made no attempt to get to his feet and was still hunched on the ground, small hissing noises escaping between his white lips.

This time Matt crawled on his belly toward his deputy, inching his way slowly, his useless leg dragging, each yard of ground its own separate ordeal, its own searing moment of hell.

After a few yards, he stopped and caught his breath. He looked back at his leg and saw that from below the knee it was sticking out at a strange angle. The intense pain never let up for even a second.

It was a bad break, and Matt knew it.

He began to crawl again, and after what seemed an eternity, he reached Festus' side. "How bad are you hit?" he asked, his voice, made hoarse by the hammering agony of his leg, a barely audible whisper.

The deputy turned, and Matt saw the answer to his question in Festus' haunted, pain-dulled eyes. "Right shoulder's broke, Matthew," the deputy gasped. "Here." He touched the front of his mackinaw, and his fingers came away glistening with blood. "An' I've got another bullet in my arm. My gun arm too."

Matt lay in silence for a few moments, thinking things through. He had not rounded up a posse to go after the McCartys because he'd believed the brothers were sure-thing killers who would give up without a fight. Back in Dodge, people would think Festus and he were still chasing after the fugitives and no one would come looking for them. Not today, maybe not tomorrow or the day after that.

Festus was badly wounded and he was losing a lot of blood. Without medical care he would be dead by morning.

There was nothing else for it — they would have to try and make it back to town.

The only question was — how?

Chapter 2

A Long Ride Home

"Festus," Matt Dillon asked, "can you ride, old-timer?"

Matt knew Festus Haggen had sand, something his deputy had proved time and again going all the way back to his rakehell days in the Texas Rangers. But the gray, strained face Festus turned to the marshal revealed the man's weakened condition.

"I dunno, Matthew," he said. "See, I feel all in, like I jes' want to lay down an' take a nap." Festus blinked like a man ready for sleep. "Let me be for a spell an' maybe then we'll ride."

The wind was again driving hard, cold and merciless, and low, dark clouds were scudding in from the west. Shadows were stealing into the hollows and folds of the surrounding land, and in the distance, the bare-limbed cottonwoods lining the creek were gradually being lost as the darkening day fell around them.

Now was not the time for kindness or for weakness either. "In this cold, fall asleep and you'll never wake up again, Festus," Matt said. Then, pretending an anger he did not feel, he snapped: "Now get on your damned feet and climb onto your mule."

"I can't do it," Festus shook his head. "Hell, Matthew, I'm shot all to pieces."

"And my leg's busted," Matt said, his voice harsh. "So we got to do it, both of us."

Festus looked at the big marshal, into eyes that had shaded from blue to a hard gunmetal gray, and he knew that Matt Dillon was leaving him no room for compromise. There could be no excuses either.

"I'll try, Matthew," Festus said finally. "But this is a hell of a thing to ask of a man who's just been shot through an' through."

The wind blowing long off the blue Sangre de Cristo Mountains three hundred miles to the west was now bringing with it a few tumbling flurries of snow. The temperature had dropped to below zero and frost clung to Festus' unkempt beard, giving him the look of a tired old man.

Groaning, the deputy struggled to his feet, then bent over from the waist for a few long moments, fighting a battle with his pain. Finally he straightened and, ashen faced, staggered to Matt. "Give me your hand, Matthew," Festus said. "Afore I attempt Ruth, I'll help you to your hoss."

The marshal shook his head, knowing that in his weakened state Festus could never support his 250 pounds. "Won't work, Festus," he said. "Bring the shotgun over here and I'll use it like a cane."

Blood loss had weakened Festus more than Matt had realized. He watched his deputy walk toward the Greener, fall, then struggle to his feet — only to fall again. Each time Festus hit the ground and got up, the snow where he'd lain was splashed scarlet. And each time he fell, his face grew paler, his eyes more glazed with pain.

Forcing back his own hammering agony, Matt began to crawl again, trying to cut down the distance between his deputy and him. He saw Festus stoop and grab the shotgun with his left hand, then turn, only to fall heavily on his back, a low moan escaping between his clenched teeth.

Matt crawled beside Festus, looked into his face, and managed a weak grin. "How you doing, old-timer?"

The deputy raised his head and nodded. "Fair to middlin', I'd say, Matthew. My shoulder is punishin' me some, but I can't feel my arm a-tall."

"Well, you lay there real still and get

your strength back," Matt said. "I'm going to try and get up."

Matt took the shotgun from Festus' hand and used it to help him climb heavily to his feet. As a shotgun, the Greener was a first-class weapon — as a crutch, it left much to be desired. Even when he leaned most of his weight on the gun, agony blazed white-hot in Matt's shattered leg. Despite the freezing chill of the day, beads of sweat popped out on his forehead and he had to bite back the groans that came, unbidden, to his lips.

He looked down at his deputy, swaying a little, and wiped sweat from his forehead with his sleeve.

"Festus," he said, "take my hand. I've got to pull you to your feet."

"I can get up," the deputy said. He tried to rise, but the effort was too much for him and he collapsed on his back.

"Like I said, take my hand," Matt ordered, sternness again edging his voice. "I swear, I never met a man that likes to lay down and nap as much as you do."

Festus stretched out his hand and Matt grabbed it. "I take after my grandpappy's side o' the family," the deputy said. "They surely loved to snooze, especially if'n there was chores to be done."

Matt pulled on Festus' hand and heaved the deputy to his feet. But Festus was unbalanced and fell heavily against the big marshal. All Matt's weight was thrown onto his broken leg and it buckled under him, and both men crashed heavily to the ground.

Matt lay flat on his back, trying not to lose consciousness, fighting against the pain that again and again smashed at him. Beside him he heard Festus moan and he turned his head to face his deputy. "Well," he said finally, "that didn't work too well, did it? I guess we'll just have to give her another whirl."

Festus nodded, his lips white. "I'm right sorry, Matthew. I reckon that was all my fault."

Matt shook his head. "I'm not tying the can on you, Festus. If anybody is to blame, it's the McCarty boys for shootin' instead of jawin', like we figured they would."

Once again Matt struggled to his feet, and this time when he helped Festus rise, the two lawmen managed to stay upright, unsteadily clinging to each other for support.

"We done it, Matthew," Festus said, managing a weak grin. "Dang me, but we done it."

"All right, you first, Festus," Matt said. "Let's get you up on Ruth."

"Matthew, I reckon your misery is worser than mine," Festus objected. "You should mount first."

Matt smiled. He pointed to the star pinned to his sheepskin coat. "What does that say?" he asked.

"I know what it says, Matthew. It says *marshal*."

Matt nodded. "It says something else — it says I'm the boss. Now get up on your mule."

Ruth, normally a belligerent, cantankerous animal, sensed that something was amiss with her rider, and for once in her life, she stood still without trying to kick or bite while Matt helped Festus into the saddle.

The struggle drained the big marshal, and when he hobbled to his bay, he laid his head against the horse's shoulder, battling the terrible pain in his leg and the waves of weakening nausea that washed over him.

Buck, already skittish over his fall, didn't like being mounted from the right side and began to dance, his head coming up, arcs of white showing in his eyes. But Matt whispered soothingly to the big horse and the bay finally settled down, sensing, like the mule had done earlier, that all was not well.

Matt put his right foot in the stirrup and swung into the saddle, moving from the hip. But he couldn't raise his leg enough. His thigh thumped against the Denver saddle's high cantle and a shocking jolt of agony jarred through his entire leg, leaving him breathless and speechless.

"You all right, Matthew?" Festus asked, kneeing his mule beside the bay, concern bunched up in his haggard face.

Matt settled himself in the saddle, his leg dangling. Unable to talk, he clenched his teeth and nodded.

Around Festus and him, flakes of snow eddied in the rising wind and the icy air smelled of raw iron. Ahead of them, the plains stretched out endlessly, coldly indifferent to man and his suffering.

It was going to be a long ride to Dodge City.

After they left Saw Log Creek behind, the two lawmen headed due south. Ahead of them lay Duck Creek, trailing willows and plum bush lining both banks, and, six miles beyond that, Dodge.

Thin ice laced the banks of the creek when they splashed across. Then they had to ride around a tangle of fallen cottonwoods, the trunks split in half from the cold of some vicious winter long past.

This was harsh, unforgiving country, made even more dangerous by the rapidly plunging temperature and the crowding gloom as the day slowly died around the two riders.

Festus had been silent for a long while, slumped in the saddle, his head bobbing to the motion of his mule. Matt rode closer to the deputy and laid a hand on his shoulder. "Festus, how you bearing up?"

When Festus turned, Matt was shocked at the change in his appearance. His face was stony gray, with deep blue shadows in the hollows of his cheeks, and fever burned hot and bright in his eyes.

"I'm plum tuckered out, Matthew," Festus whispered. "What say we hole up for a while and take us a rest?"

Matt shook his head. "There's nowhere around here to hole up, Festus. Besides, my leg is swollen to twice its size. If you get down off that mule, I'll never be able to get you back up on her again."

"I'm so sleepy, Matthew." The deputy mumbled. "I need to rest, is all . . . jes' rest for a spell. . . ."

Matt realized the danger. If Festus fell

asleep and tumbled off his mule, he was done for. Matt had the Greener across his saddle horn but the lower part of his leg from the knee down was so grotesquely swollen he wondered that his pants hadn't split. Even using the scattergun as a crutch, he would be unable to stand. All he could do would be to ride to Dodge for help, but by the time help arrived, Festus would have frozen to death.

As the day rapidly shaded into evening, the sky was darkening, building black clouds stretching from horizon to horizon like gigantic sheets of curled lead. Matt's breath smoked in the icy air and the wind-driven snowflakes were so cold they stung his face like a swarm of angry bees.

Festus' head dropped lower, his chin on his chest, and his eyes closed.

"Wake up!" Matt yelled. "Damn it, Festus. Don't you go to sleep on me."

The deputy's head jerked erect, but his eyes were half closed, the lids drooping. "I'll try, Matthew. I'll surely try."

Desperately Matt racked his brain for a solution, then found one, though he told himself it was woefully inadequate at best. "We'll sing," he said. "Both of us."

Festus shook his head, trying to get his fogged mind to work. "Sing?"

"Sing," Matt said. "So long as you're singing, I know you're awake."

"But I don't know no songs," Festus said. "Never could carry a tune, so I've never been what you might call a singin' man."

"Well, I'll do the singing then. Just you follow along."

Matt broke into song, his deep, flat baritone defying the rising wind that tried its best to snatch the words from his lips.

Goodbye, Old Paint.
  I'm a-leavin' Cheyenne.
Goodbye, Old Paint.
  I'm a-leavin' Cheyenne.
I'm a-leavin' Cheyenne.
  I'm off to Montan'.
Goodbye, Old Paint.
  I'm a-leavin' Cheyenne.

Festus groaned and shook his head. "Matthew, that's the worse singin' I ever heard in my life," he said. "You'd drive a coyote to suicide."

"Well, if you don't like my singing, let me hear you do better." Matt smiled. "Now have at it, Festus, good and loud."

The deputy's cracked, tuneless voice joined with Matt's, much to the displeasure of Festus' mule, who tossed her head and brayed loudly, an equal match, Matt decided, for the singing of the two humans.

They rode on as the night and the snow fell around them, a tall man on a tall horse, his strong right arm supporting a smaller man, who rode a rangy mule. Out in the prairie the coyotes were calling and the sky was now black as ink, showing no stars.

But by the time Dodge came in sight, Matt was holding his deputy in the saddle and Festus' voice had become a hoarse, exhausted whisper. He was gamely trying to carry the song, but the words no longer made sense.

"Paint . . . Old Paint . . . Cheyenne . . . Old Paint . . ."

Matt reined up outside the Dodge House, and within moments, willing hands lifted Festus and him from their saddles.

"Be careful with him," Matt warned as several men carried the deputy into the hotel. "He's in a bad way."

"Marshal," a white-bearded oldster threw over his shoulder, "I don't know if'n you've noticed, but you're in a bad way your ownself."

Chapter 3

A Woman's Strength

"Matt, your leg is so swollen, I'll have to cut off the boot before I can do anything else." Dr. Galen Adams looked closely at the marshal's leg, then shook his head. "It's a bad break."

"Doc, that boot was custom-made in El Paso, Texas," Matt protested. "Cost fifty dollars a pair."

"Custom made in El Paso, Texas, huh?" Doc scowled. "Fifty dollars a pair, is it? Then tell me, Marshal Dillon, how much your leg is worth because if that boot doesn't come off I can't put the broken bones back together."

Matt's head thumped back onto his pillow. "All right, cut if off, Doc." He hesitated a split second, then added: "The boot, I mean."

Doc nodded. "Figured you'd say that."

As the physician raised his scalpel and began to work on the tough leather of the boot, Matt asked: "How is Festus?"

"He'll be all right," Doc answered. "Dr.

Johnson is working on him."

Matt's head jerked off the pillow. "But Irv Johnson is a horse doctor."

Doc Adams nodded. "And an excellent one too. He's also cut as many bullets out of humans as I have. Besides, I always said Festus was as stubborn as an old mule, so he's in good hands."

Seeing the doubt in Matt's face, Doc sighed and stopped his work with the scalpel. "As soon as I get this leg straightened and splinted, I'll check on Festus. But, as I told you, when it comes to bullet wounds, Irv Johnson is one of the best."

From out in the hallway, Matt heard a girl's voice raised in alarm and the sound of another sobbing.

Doc smiled and inclined his head toward the door. "The ladies from across the tracks are already assembling. I guess they got the word about Festus."

At the insistence of Mayor Kelley, Festus regularly patrolled the respectable part of town, though Matt reckoned he spent more time drinking brandy in lace-curtained parlors with the fashionable Dodge City belles and their mothers than he did policing the streets.

The deputy's tales of his derring-do in the Rangers had made him a hero to the womenfolk over there, and Matt was sure Festus would soon be playing the role of brave wounded warrior to the hilt.

Feeling a little left out, he asked, "Where's Kitty, Doc?"

Doc Adams allowed himself another rare smile. "Don't worry, Matt. She'll be here. I told her to stay away until I get this leg treated." Then, realizing his reputation for crankiness might be slipping, he added quickly: "I can't abide being surrounded by caterwauling females when I'm trying to work."

Doc eased off Matt's boot and his expert fingers probed the marshal's injured leg. Finally he said: "Matt, both your lower leg bones — what we doctors call the tibia and fibula — are broken. Seems like clean breaks but to align those bones back into place I'm going to have to pull on your leg mighty hard." The physician looked down at his patient. "I won't lie to you, Matt. It's going to hurt."

Matt nodded. "I've seen a broke leg fixed before. You go ahead and do what you have to, Doc."

Doc Adams reached into the pocket of his coat and produced a pint of rye whiskey. "Take a good slug of this. It will help some."

Matt did as he was told, the rye immediately spreading a comforting fire through his belly. Outside the night lay thick over Dodge, and the oil lamp on the table near Matt's bed threw flickering yellow-and-orange light into the dark corners of the room. From a nearby saloon, a piano dropped hesitant, fragile notes into the quiet, and from a much greater distance away, out on the snow-covered prairie, the coyotes were still talking.

Doc took off his coat, rolled up his sleeves and said: "Matt, hold on to the back of the bed. When I start pulling, I don't want you to move with me."

Matt, his eyes wary, grasped the brass rails at each side of his head.

"Ready?" Doc asked.

The marshal nodded, resigned to his fate. "As I'll ever be."

"Then let's get it done."

Doc grabbed Matt's leg by the ankle and pulled. The pain was shocking, a searing thunderbolt of agony like a strong man had crashed a sledgehammer into Matt's shin. He gasped back a groan, and from close by, he heard a high-pitched shriek. Had that cry been forced out of him? Another shriek. Then another, louder this time and more drawn-out.

The bed was moving.

The shrill, screeching shrieks were coming from rusted iron wheels skidding and scraping across the scarred timber floor of the room.

Doc pulled again, his teeth gritted, and Matt saw beads of sweat pop out on the physician's forehead. Every time Doc yanked on Matt's leg, he pulled the bed with him, and at each pull, Matt's suffering grew. Doc, stepping backward, crashed into the nightstand and the water pitcher and washbasin tumbled to the floor, smashing into a hundred pieces.

When the bed was halfway across the room, Doc cursed under his breath and eased Matt's leg back onto the mattress.

He brushed sweat from his eyes with his forearm and said: "Matt, you have a horseman's leg. The muscles are so strong I can't pull it straight because the bed keeps moving with me. I need some help."

"So do I, Doc," Matt said weakly, struggling to smile as scorching pain hammered at him. "A few times there, I was about to get up from this here bed and make a run for it."

"You wouldn't have gotten far," Doc said, his voice dry as parchment.

Doc walked quickly to the door,

crunching though the remains of the broken pitcher and yelled: "You women out there, quit your caterwauling and round up a couple of strong men — quick! And bring Kitty Russell here."

Within a few minutes two men walked into Matt's room. One was the night desk clerk, the other a huge rancher called Chet Lagrange, a man Matt knew only by sight.

Kitty was right behind them and her shocked eyes took in the situation at a glance. She ran to Matt and put her head on his chest. "Matt," she whispered, "I've been so worried. Are you all right?"

"No, he's not all right, woman," Doc snapped. "I have to get that leg straightened out or he'll be crippled for life." The physician nodded to his two helpers. "You men grab the back of the bed and don't let it move." He turned. "Kitty, it's up to you to hold Matt down. When the pain hits him again, I don't want him trying to climb out of that bed."

"Doc, maybe I should hold down on the marshal," Lagrange said. "I'm a lot stronger than Miss Kitty."

Doc shook his head. "Chet, if Matt Dillon wants to get out of that bed you couldn't hold him. In fact all three of us men couldn't hold him — but Kitty can."

The clerk and Lagrange grabbed the back of the bed and braced themselves for what was to come. Kitty laid her head on Matt's chest, her tears staining his shirt, her hands pressing on his wide shoulders.

"This time, Matt," Doc said. "This time we get it done." He grabbed the marshal's foot and gave the leg a powerful yank.

A split second before a tidal wave of pain swept over him, Matt heard a snap as the bones slammed into place. The pain followed close after, and he arched his back and bit back a scream. Then, mercifully, he lost consciousness and knew no more.

Matt Dillon woke to gray daylight.

He opened his eyes and for a few moments stared at the ceiling, trying to remember where he was and what had happened to him.

Then he remembered.

He raised his head from the pillow and looked down at his leg. Doc Adams had expertly splinted the leg from knee to ankle with pine boards and had bound the boards together with medical tape.

With a pang of regret, Matt noted that not only was his custom boot ruined, but his best pair of pants was slit to the knee and he had a hole in his sock.

He heard a soft creak and turned his head. Kitty tossed off the blanket that covered her, rose from her chair and stepped quickly to his bedside.

"How are you feeling?" she asked.

Matt ignored Kitty's question and asked a couple of his own. "What time is it? Have you been here all night?"

"I think it's about ten," Kitty answered. "And yes, I've been here all night. Somebody had to be around to take care of you. And I'd rather it was me than some other woman."

"Thank you."

"Doc left you a set of crutches," Kitty said, "though I don't think you'll be using them for a while. You need to rest that leg for a few days."

Matt grinned and shook his head. "Kitty, I never was much of a one for lying in bed. I plan on using those crutches to make my rounds tonight."

"We'll see," Kitty said, but Matt could recognize in the determined set of her chin that she had no intention of letting him do anything of the kind.

"How's Festus?" Matt asked, letting go of the matter, at least for now.

Kitty smiled. "A bevy of ladies took in their wounded hero's breakfast about an hour ago. If all the giggling I heard from Festus' room is anything to go by, I'd say he's feeling a lot better."

Kitty took Matt's hand in hers. She then kneeled beside the bed and laid her head on his chest. They stayed that way for a long time, saying nothing, communicating a thousand things without a single word of talk. . . .

But the sudden roar of angry guns shattered their quiet. A few moments later the door of the hotel banged open, and a man's voice yelled something Matt couldn't make out. Other doors slammed and he heard people hollering questions. Then booted feet pounded on the stairs and knuckles rapped urgently on Matt's door.

Kitty rose and opened the door and Chet Lagrange stormed inside. "Marshal," the rancher hollered, his breath coming in short, fast gasps, "the Cattleman's Bank has just been robbed." His eyes wild, he gulped down a chunk of air, then added: "The bandits got away clean and they've left men dead on the street."

Chapter 4

The Big Snow

Matt struggled to rise from the bed, but Kitty pushed him back. "Matt, you can't go after those robbers. Your leg needs time to heal."

Lagrange stepped beside the bed, a tall, wide-shouldered man with a hard-boned face and ice blue eyes that betrayed both ruthlessness and determination.

"The lady is right, Marshal. Deputize me now and I'll round up a posse. We'll run down them robbers."

"I'm coming with you," Matt said, throwing the blanket off his legs.

"How do you plan on doing that?" Kitty asked, her eyes blazing. "You can't even walk, let alone ride a horse." She kneeled and asked: "Why, Matt? Why not let Chet handle it?"

"Why? Because if I don't go after those men every two-bit outlaw for hundreds of miles around will figure he can get away with robbery and murder in Matt Dillon's town." He swung his legs off the bed. "I'm not about to let that happen." The big marshal looked up at Lagrange. "Chet, consider yourself deputized. Round up the posse, as many men as you can find, and I'll meet you in the street in a few minutes."

The big rancher cast one doubtful look at Matt's leg, then hurried out of the room.

"Kitty," Matt said, "bring me those crutches."

The woman opened her mouth to object, realized the uselessness of doing so, and brought the crutches to the bed.

After a few moments' struggle, Matt managed to climb to his feet and tuck the crutches under his armpits. "Kitty, where's my gun belt?" he asked.

Kitty stepped to the dresser, picked up the cartridge belt and holstered Colt and brought them to him. "Matt, this is madness," she said. "You can't ride."

"I have it to do, Kitty," the marshal answered, buckling on the gun belt. "I owe it to this town and I owe it to myself. Just call it the rent I pay for being here."

His crutches thudding on the pine boards, Matt made his way to the door. Kitty stepped in front of him and opened it wide, knowing that further argument was useless. She handed him his sheepskin coat. "At least let me help you put this on," she said. "It's cold out there."

With Kitty's help, Matt shrugged into the coat, then, unused to crutches, he awkwardly made his way along the hallway to the landing. He thumped past several rooms, anxious faces appearing at the doors as he passed — and then he saw the stairs.

He'd forgotten about the stairs! For a healthy man, a flight of stairs was nothing, but for a man on crutches, they were a major obstacle, a difficult and treacherous slope plunging steeply away from him.

Matt hesitated, and Kitty, seeing his uncertainty, stepped beside him. "I'll help you," she said. "Lean on me."

The big marshal shook his head. "Kitty, if I fall we'll both go tumbling down those stairs." He managed a grin. "Wait for me at the bottom. If I slip and fall, you can help me get on my feet again."

Kitty tried one last time. "Matt, go back to your room. Let Chet Lagrange head out after the bank robbers."

"Do as I say, Kitty," Matt said, his voice even, understanding the woman's concern. "Wait for me at the bottom." Then, attempting to make light of the ordeal facing him, he added: "I might come down mighty fast."

The tears staining Kitty's eyes were replaced by a flare of anger. "Go ahead then, Matt Dillon. Break your fool neck."

She rushed down the steps, walked quickly past the clerk's desk and put her hand on the door handle. Kitty hesitated there for a few moments, her back stiff. Then she turned and walked to the bottom of the stairs again.

"If you fall, Matt," she said, looking up at him, "I'll be here to pick you up."

It took Matt several minutes to negotiate the stairs, hesitantly, one step at a time, like a child learning to walk. The Dodge House, heated by inadequate wood-burning stoves, was cold, but Matt was sweating heavily when he finally reached the bottom step.

Kitty opened the door for him and he thudded outside onto the boardwalk. Further along Front Street a crowd had gathered outside the Cattleman's Bank, and Percy Crump the undertaker, with his vulture's instinct for death, was already standing by, a tape measure around his neck like the stole of a melancholy and demented priest.

Matt looked up and down the street but

saw no sign of Chet Lagrange and the posse. He stopped a man passing on the boardwalk and asked after the big rancher.

"Marshal, the posse just left with Chet Lagrange leading them," the man answered. He pointed to the wooden bridge over the Arkansas. "Saw a half dozen riders cross there an' head south after them robbers, oh, a couple of minutes ago I guess."

They'd gone without him!

Matt cursed under his breath. He was going to have some hard words with Lagrange when the man got back. The big marshal turned and stomped along the boardwalk toward the livery stable, his crutches pounding angrily on the rough pine slats.

Kitty hurried beside him, shivering as she drew her blue velvet cloak more tightly around her shoulders. The temperature was dropping fast and the sky was black, covered with lowering clouds. Despite the hour, the twilight gloom of dusk had descended on Dodge and fretful flurries of snow tossed in a threatening wind.

When he reached the Cattleman's Bank, Matt stopped. Silas Morgan, the slight, frail teller, lay sprawled out dead on the boardwalk, a Smith & Wesson .38 still clutched in his hand, the front of his chest splashed with blood. A few yards away the body of Tom Bodie was stretched out facedown close to his fallen rifle.

Morgan was married and over at his modest house across the tracks were his thin, plain wife and three small children. Tom Bodie, a veteran of the War Between the States, had worn a cowtown lawman's star a couple of times before retiring to the hardware business. He'd fought Comanches and Apaches in his day and he was not a man to take lightly.

Both Morgan and Bodie were decent, upright citizens of Dodge and Matt felt their loss keenly.

Jed Owens was standing outside the door of the Cattleman's, his face under his walrus mustache and thick red sideburns the color of chalk.

Matt stomped his way to the side of the banker and asked: "How did it happen, Jed?"

Owens turned to Matt and blinked once or twice like a man waking from a bad dream. "Huh?"

"How did it happen?" Matt asked again.

The banker stood for a few moments, collecting his thoughts, then said: "They hit us at ten o'clock, just as we were opening. Took almost fifty thousand dollars. Cleaned me out, Matt. Cleaned me out and ruined a lot of people in this town."

The marshal knew well what a bank robbery meant to a town like Dodge. Most of the bank's money came from small investors and, in many cases, represented their life savings. When their bank was robbed, they lost everything.

Matt nodded to the bodies lying in the street. "Silas Morgan and Tom Bodie, what happened?"

Owens, his white face lumpy, took a deep breath and shook his head, as though trying to rid himself of an unpleasant memory. "When the robbers left, Silas grabbed his gun and went after them. He didn't even get a shot off before they gunned him down. Tom ran out of the hardware store with his rifle, yelled at them to hold up and then they shot him."

"Recognize any of them, Jed?"

"There were six or seven of them, Matt, and I don't remember their faces." The banker hesitated. "Well, all except one, the man who killed Silas and Tom." Owens' fingers went to his left cheekbone. "He was a big man, almost as tall as you, and he had a deep gouge right across here, like maybe he'd been hit by a bullet one time."

"Did he walk with a limp, Jed? Favor his right leg some?"

The banker shook his head. "That I didn't notice. You think you might know him?"

"Maybe. There's an outlaw answers that description, goes by the name of Scar Henry. He runs with a fast gunman out of Indian Territory called Deacon Waters." Matt nodded, thinking. "Could be him," he said finally. "If it was Henry who robbed your bank, they don't come any worse, and Deacon Waters is no bargain either. He's killed more than his share."

"You going after the robbers, Matt?" Owens asked. "The posse already left."

"I know. But I'll catch up to them." Matt turned and called out to the hovering undertaker. "Percy, get these dead men off the damn street and set them up decent." He turned to Owens again. "Jed, I'd take it as a favor if you'd break the news to Mrs. Morgan."

The banker nodded. "I'll do it. And I'll take my own missus with me. At a time like this, Jane Morgan will want another woman close."

"Jed, if it's all the same to you, I'd like to come with you," Kitty said. "If you think Jane won't mind a saloon owner in her home."

"I think she'll be right glad to have you there, Miss Kitty," Owens replied. "And the missus and me will too."

Kitty turned to the marshal. "I guess I still can't get you to change your mind."

"Not a chance." Matt smiled.

"Then . . . be careful."

"Count on it."

As Matt struggled on his crutches toward the livery stable, the wind picked up and the snow fell heavier, tumbling in shifting white clouds around him. It had grown even colder in the past few minutes, and he stopped and pulled the fleece collar of his coat higher around his ears.

Matt glanced uneasily at the sky. Billowing black clouds shading to gray at the edges looked like gigantic mountains thousands of feet high, grim, ominous peaks cut through by deep draws and arroyos. Matt's breath smoked in the bitter cold as he made his laborious way toward the stable, the now ravaging wind tugging and tearing at him, bullying him with its strength.

The morning light was dying around him, replaced by the darkness of the gathering storm, and along Front Street, lamps were being lit in the saloons, their windows glowing like wide, fearful eyes.

Matt thumped and bumped his way into the barn and Lou Carlson, the stable hand, stepped out of his small office by the door. "Heard you was all stove up, Marshal," he said. "How you feeling with that broke leg an' all?"

"Pretty fair, Lou," Matt answered. "I need my horse."

"You heading out after them bank robbers?"

Matt nodded. "Yes. Now get my horse, Lou."

Carlson's glance slid over Matt's shoulder to the door and he shook his head. "You don't need ol' Buck this morning, Marshal." The man's smile was without humor. "You ain't going anyplace."

"You plan on trying to stop me, Lou?" Matt asked, his voice ominously low and hard-edged.

Carlson motioned in the direction of the door. "Hell no, not me — but that is."

Matt turned awkwardly on his crutches and looked outside. What he saw shocked him. Thickly falling snow was cartwheeling past the barn door, driven by a howling wind off the plains. The frame building shook and creaked under the pounding of the gusting blasts, and behind him, Matt heard a horse whinny in alarm and kick at the door to its stall.

The big snow Matt had predicted to Festus had arrived, a killer blizzard bent on turning the plains into a cold, white hell.

Matt was aware of Carlson stepping beside him. "I don't reckon your posse is going anywhere either, Marshal," the man said. "Now I come to think on it, neither are those bank robbers."

Chapter 5

Return of the Outlaws

The gunfighting lawman's instinct for impending danger ran strong in Matt Dillon and now he heeded its insistent clamor. Supporting all his weight on the crutch under his left arm, he passed the other one to Carlson. "Lou," he said, "take this."

"What you want me to do with it, Marshal?" the man asked.

"I don't know. Stow it somewhere. I won't be needing it."

Lou Carlson was also a man of the West and he understood the significance of the big marshal's gesture. A lawman can't draw a gun with a crutch under his arm.

"You think those outlaws will head back to Dodge?" Carlson asked, taking the crutch.

Matt nodded. "Lou, I'm sure of it. Until this storm blows itself out, they have no place else to go. They sure can't stay out there on the plains."

"You can keep the posse together when it gets back," Carlson suggested. "Lay in wait for them killers."

"Maybe," Matt said, his face bleak. "But those posse members are mostly married men, and they'll want to weather out a storm like this with their families." He turned to the stable hand. "I guess we'll just have to wait and see."

Matt did not want Carlson to notice his concern, but secretly he was worried.

The six or seven citizens of Dodge in the posse would be tough and as game as they come, all of them experienced with guns. But if it really was Scar Henry and Deacon Waters who'd robbed the bank, they'd be badly outmatched. From what Matt had heard, both outlaws were fast and deadly gunmen, and he was certain the others with them would be no bargain either.

If Henry came back, looking for a place to hole up, he'd be primed and ready to hunt trouble and that would mean more men dead on the street — maybe a sight more.

Matt shook his head. Crippled as he was, he'd have to face Scar Henry. That was what Dodge was paying him for, and he would not earn his wages with the blood of other men.

Maybe he'd get lucky and nail both Henry and Waters and the rest of the bunch would give up. But it was a mighty big maybe, and it gave Matt no comfort. The big marshal headed out of the livery into the storm. Driving snow and wind tore at him as he struggled on one crutch along the slippery boardwalk toward Newly O'Brien's gun store.

O'Brien was behind his counter working on the action of a Winchester when Matt stepped inside and brushed snow from his coat.

"Blowing out there, Marshal," the gunsmith said. "I reckon we're in for a time."

Matt nodded. "I'd say so, Newly." He stomped to the counter and O'Brien rose and laid the rifle back on the rack behind him.

"Sorry about the leg," O'Brien said. "Broken leg like that can wear on a man."

Matt was not hunting sympathy, so he made no reply. He ordered a couple of boxes each of .45 and .44.40 shells and a box of double-aught buck for the Greener.

"Expecting a war, Marshal?" O'Brien said, smiling as he stacked the boxes on the counter. "Them bank robbers maybe?"

"They could come back, Newly," Matt answered. "This big snow could drive them in, and when they get here, I plan to be ready."

"If you need help, count on me," O'Brien said. "I got my rifle."

"I set store by that offer, Newly," Matt said. "When the ball opens, if it does, I may come calling on you."

"Anytime," the gunsmith said. "All you have to do is ask, Marshal."

After he left O'Brien's store, Matt headed for his office. He'd sleep there on the cot. He'd had his fill of stairs for a spell.

As he pounded his way along the board-walk, the day was cold, colder than he ever thought it could be, and the snow was drawing a shifting veil across Front Street. The saloons and other buildings seemed to be huddling together for protection from the storm, the thick snow on their roofs like white nightcaps, giving them the look of tired, creaky old men preparing for a long winter sleep.

The shrieking wind tore at Matt, threat-ening to knock him over, and his face felt raw, his fingers numb. Around him, the street was empty. No one ventured out into the blizzard, which was baring white fangs. Everywhere the snow lay a foot thick and it was already starting to drift, piling up against the sides of buildings in a series of icy peaks and valleys.

Somewhere out there in the storm were Chet Lagrange and the posse — and the bank robbers. For both parties, Matt decided grimly, time was fast running out.

As he passed the telegraph office, Barney Danches opened his door and hailed him. "Marshal, the telegraph is out," the agent said. "Line must be down somewhere." Danches waved a hand that encompassed the town and the sky. "The storm you know."

Matt nodded his thanks, trying to make light of it. But Danches' news added to his worry. Without the telegraph, Dodge was cut off from the outside world. If the trains stopped running, and that was a real possibility, the town would be totally isolated.

And there was another if. What if Scar Henry and his gang really did decide to wait out the blizzard in Dodge? Matt could expect no help from the outside. It would be just him and them — another thought that offered him no solace.

He reached his office, opened the door and struggled inside. It was still shy of noon, but the office was in darkness and Matt lit the oil lamp hanging from the ceiling.

Outside the fury of the blizzard was growing, and when he looked out, he could not see the opposite side of the street, just the faint glow of the Long Branch windows, like dim lanterns seen through a thick, swirling fog.

Matt fed shells into his Winchester and then loaded the Greener. He placed both guns back in the rack, took down the Henry he and Festus kept as a spare rifle and thumbed thirteen .44.40 cartridges into the magazine.

He replaced the Henry and smiled grimly to himself. Newly O'Brien had asked him if he was expecting a war. The answer to that question was that he didn't know what to expect . . . but if the war came, he was as ready as he could possibly be.

Now the next move was up to the bank robbers.

Matt ate a can of beans from the meager supplies he kept in his office and had coffee boiling when he glanced out the window and saw the posse ride into Dodge. The men were bent over in their saddles, heads down against the force of the wind, and both men and horses were covered in snow, looking like pale ghost riders.

The marshal had promised himself that he would have some hard words with Chet

Lagrange, but the thought of struggling through the storm on one crutch, dragging his left leg, the foot protected only by a sock with a hole in it, stopped him. Best to let it wait until the blizzard blew itself out. In the meantime, Matt decided, he would nurse his righteous wrath to keep it warm.

Stomping closer to the window, a cup of coffee in his hand, Matt again looked outside. It was hard to tell because of the driving snow, but he thought he could make out the dim shape of a body draped across a horse.

Had Lagrange caught up to the robbers and killed one of them before the blizzard hit? It was possible, because from what he heard about Lagrange, the big rancher was a hard-driving, capable man.

Making up his mind, Matt laid his cup on the desk, struggled into his sheepskin and settled his hat on his head. Blizzard or no, he would have to talk to Lagrange and check on the identity of the dead man.

Matt opened the office door and struggled outside. When he tried to close the door again, the force of the wind tore the knob from his hand and the door slammed open against the wall. He let it go. A wide overhang sheltered the front of the office and very little snow would blow inside, or so he hoped.

As the big marshal made his way across the street, he saw the shadowy figures of a couple of riders leading horses toward the livery stable. The dead man was still draped across his saddle outside the Long Branch, but everyone else seemed to have stepped inside.

The blizzard hammered at Matt and had plastered a thick layer of snow over the front of his sheepskin coat by the time he made his way to the hitching rail outside the saloon. He stopped and studied the pale blue face of the dead man. This was no outlaw! The features were frozen, mustache and eyebrows covered in ice crystals, but they were unmistakable — it was Ephraim Jenkins, one of the Alhambra Saloon's night bartenders.

Jenkins must have been one of the volunteers who had ridden in Chet Lagrange's posse.

Matt stood beside the dead man for a few moments, the snow falling around him. He knew Jenkins well and liked the man. It looked like Lagrange had stumbled into a gunfight with the outlaws and Jenkins had been killed. But what of the outlaws? Were they all dead?

There was one way to find out. Matt struggled onto the boardwalk, slipped on an icy patch of snow and had to fight hard to regain his balance. Stepping more carefully now, he stomped toward the door of the saloon, unbuttoned his coat and limped inside.

After the freezing cold of outside the saloon was warm, heated by several large potbellied stoves. Sitting at one of the stoves, his boots off, wiggling his toes to the heat, was a tall man with a terrible scar across his left cheekbone. That man was Scar Henry.

Matt stopped in his tracks and pushed his coat away from the star on his vest as he took in the situation at a glance.

Kitty and Sam Noonan stood behind the bar, their faces strained, wide, unblinking eyes revealing their fear. A downcast Chet Lagrange and his posse, a couple of them nursing wounds, sat at several tables scattered around the saloon. At each table stood an outlaw with a Winchester.

At a table near Scar Henry sat a slim man with quiet blue eyes in a hawk face, toying with a deck of cards in his hands. The man had given Matt a slight smile when he'd walked in, but it was the cold, confident and knowing smile of a coiled rattler. Matt knew this could only be Deacon Waters, said to be the fastest gun west of the Mississippi. Waters was a cool, pitiless gunman who had killed eight men, one of them not long ago, Dutchy Long, a skilled gunfighter out of Las Cruces with a big reputation.

Waters, Matt decided, was a man to be reckoned with.

Scar Henry, tall and large boned, with shaggy black hair and a straggling, untrimmed mustache doing little to enhance his ruined face, turned his head and looked the marshal up and down. "Now what the hell are you doing here, lawman, an' you with a broke leg an' all?" he asked.

Matt's reply was to brush back his coat and pull his gun. "Scar Henry, I'm arresting you and all of your gang for murder and bank robbery."

"You don't say." Henry grinned, completely at ease but his scarred face revealed the cruel, ugly look of something scaly that had just crawled out of a shell. Henry turned to Waters, who had not made a move of any kind but was still smiling slightly, the deck of cards turning slowly in nerveless hands. "Hey, Deke, the lawman's here to arrest us."

One of the outlaws standing guard on

the posse guffawed and Waters allowed his smile to widen. "Then I guess we should give ourselves up and go over to the jail and all play patty-cake," he said.

"Henry," Matt said, his voice low and level, "get up from that chair and drop your gun belt. And that goes for the rest of you."

Henry rose slowly to his feet. He wore black jeans, a filthy red flannel shirt and a ragged sheepskin coat. A bone-handled Colt in a cross-draw holster rode at the front of his left hip, and Matt saw to his disgust that the handle was notched — a cheap tinhorn's trick.

"I don't think you're gonna arrest anybody, Marshal," Henry said.

Then Matt saw it, just the slight slide of Henry's eyes away from his face to his left shoulder. Matt tried to turn, but slow and awkward on his crutch, he didn't make it. He heard Kitty scream: "No!" Then suddenly the crutch was kicked out from under him. Unable to support himself on his broken leg, Matt fell heavily on his back, his gun skidding across the floor of the saloon.

Amazingly fast for a man of his size, Henry limped to Matt on his socked feet. He looked down at the marshal, a sneer on his lips. "Like I told you, you're arresting nobody — not now, not ever," he said. The man studied Matt's face for a few moments, then asked: "What's your name?"

"Matt Dillon. And I swear to you, Henry, you'll have cause to remember it."

Beyond Henry, Matt saw Waters' head snap up, something in the gunman's eyes telling him that his name meant something to him.

"You called me Scar," Henry said. "I don't like that name. Nobody calls me that name, especially some two-bit lawman." He brought the heel of his foot down hard on Matt's broken leg and the big marshal gasped as shocking pain hammered at him. Vaguely, as though from a long distance away, he heard Henry say: "Call me that name again and I'll break your other damn leg."

Kitty ran from behind the bar and kneeled at Matt's side. She looked up at Henry, anger flaming in her face. "Leave him alone, you filthy animal!" she cried.

Henry threw back his head and laughed, his black eyes devouring her, burning with lust. "Little lady, come bedtime you're gonna find out just what a filthy animal I can be," he said.

"I'd die before I'd let a creature like you

touch me," Kitty snapped.

"That," Henry said, "can be arranged."

A bearded man in a snow-spattered duster stepped beside Henry. Matt looked up at him, remembering his face. This was the outlaw who had kicked his crutch away, one of the two men he'd seen leading horses to the livery stable.

"Want me to plug him for you now, Dave?" he asked Henry. "It ain't no trouble."

The big outlaw shook his head. "Nah, maybe when we pull out of here. Maybe sooner. It depends on whether or not he behaves himself." He roughly pushed Kitty aside, put a hand under Matt's arm and said to the other man: "Tom, help me get him to his feet."

The man called Tom did as he was told, and he and Henry pulled Matt off the floor and slammed his back against the bar. Another outlaw picked up Matt's crutch and propped it beside Henry.

Henry shoved his face close to Matt's, so close the marshal could smell the outlaw's rank breath. "Now you listen to me and listen good, Dillon. Me and the boys plan to wait out this storm. Then we're gonna take up a collection at the three other banks in town. After that, we'll ride out of here." He waved a hand toward Kitty. "And I plan to take her with me."

Henry grabbed Matt by the front of his coat and pulled him closer. "Now, if anybody tries to interfere with us — I mean you, your maiden aunt, anyone else — I'll start killing these prisoners." He pointed his finger at Kitty. "Seeing as how she's so sweet on you an' all, maybe I'll change my mind about keeping her. Maybe I'll start with her."

"Henry," Matt gritted through clenched teeth, "touch her and I'll hunt you down and kill you." He looked over Henry's shoulders to the other men in the saloon. "I'll kill every last one of you."

Henry grinned. "Big talk from a one-legged man." He pushed Matt away from him. "You just remember what I told you. Anybody meddles with me or any of my boys and I start shooting." Henry stepped back. "Now get the hell out of here and spread the word."

Matt was bucking a stacked deck and he knew it. Swallowing his pride, he realized this was a time to bend with the prevailing wind. There was nothing he could do right now to save Kitty and the others and take back his town. That would have to come later. But concerning the how of it and the timing of it, he had no idea.

The big marshal reached out to take his crutch, but Henry snatched it away from him. "Hop out of here or crawl out, it don't make no never mind to me," he said, a vicious smile tugging at his small, cruel mouth.

One of the outlaws guffawed, and a couple of others gathered around Henry to watch the fun.

Matt stood still, uncertain. Kitty rushed to his side. "I'll help you back to your office," she said.

"No, you won't," Henry said. He grabbed Kitty's arm and pulled her roughly away from Matt. "I told him to crawl out of here."

Chet Lagrange rose angrily from his chair and walked quickly toward Henry, his fists clenched. "Damn you! Let the marshal alone," he yelled. "Can't you leave a man his pride?"

Scar Henry turned and drew and his gun spat flame. Hit dead center, Lagrange staggered back a few steps, then fell on his face. The man struggled to raise his head and he looked up at Matt.

"Marshal," he whispered, "I'm sorry. I led them into an ambush. They were laying for us. We didn't —" Lagrange's head sank to the floor and suddenly all the life was gone from him.

Henry grinned, reloaded his Colt and turned to Matt. "Call that my affydavy," he said. "When I say I'll start shooting, I really do mean it."

A fierce anger building in him, Matt snapped: "Henry, you're a sorry piece of murdering trash. I'll see you hang for this."

"Don't count on it," Henry said. He pointed his gun at Matt. "Now get down on your belly and crawl on out of this saloon."

"Aw, Dave, give the man his crutch and let him be."

Deacon Waters rose from his table and stepped through drifting gray powder smoke beside Henry. Waters was not much above middle height, a slim, compact man with startling blue eyes who wore two Smith & Wesson Russians hanging in finely carved holsters.

"Give me the crutch, Dave," he said.

"Deke, are you crossing me?" Henry asked, a dangerous edge to his voice. "I don't like to be crossed, even by you."

The gunman shook his head. "You're the boss, Dave — you know that. I just don't want to see a fellow professional crawl, not today." Waters' eyes searched Matt's face.

"Heard about you, Dillon. You rode with some pretty wild ones a spell back."

"That was a long time ago," Matt said. "Later I chose my side."

Waters nodded, his eyes moving to the star on Matt's chest. "Yeah, I guess you did." He took the crutch from Henry and handed it to the marshal. Then he picked up Matt's Colt from the floor and shoved it into his holster. "Call this professional courtesy." He smiled. "You and me, we're two of a kind."

Matt shook his head, anger still riding him. "We're not two of a kind, Waters. You're murdering trash, just like the rest of them."

Henry let out a wild whoop of laughter. "Still want to give him the crutch and his gun, Deke boy?"

Waters' smile had slipped but his eyes were level and calm. "This one time, Dillon," he said. "This once and never again." He nodded toward the door. "Now get out of here while you still can."

As Matt stomped to the door, he heard Henry say behind him: "You're making a mistake, Deke. You humble a two-bit lawman like that, you humble him so bad he never has the gall to show his face around his jerkwater burg again."

"Don't you fret none, Dave," Waters said quietly. "If it was a mistake, I'll rectify it right quick."

Chapter 6

Festus Makes a Choice

The snow was falling even heavier, driven by a relentless wind that moaned and sighed along Front Street. When Matt trudged onto the boardwalk outside the Long Branch and struggled, head bent, past Newly O'Brien's gun store, the bouncing wooden sign hanging on iron chains above his head screeched and banged and the closed window shutters rattled restlessly on their hinges.

It was still full day, but darkness had crowded into Dodge. The snow, drifting now, had failed to transform the town into a thing of beauty. If anything it had made it shabbier, uglier, like an ancient, wrinkled crone all dressed up in a white wedding gown.

Still angry, his pride hurt, Matt struggled toward the Dodge House. He had thought briefly of bursting back into the Long Branch, gun blazing, trying to drop Henry and Waters and as many of the rest before he was hit. But he had dismissed the idea.

They'd be expecting a play like that and be waiting for him. He'd be gunned down as soon as he entered the saloon, and his death would do nothing to help Kitty and the rest of the people of Dodge.

There had to be another way — if he could find it.

But right now Matt's main concern was to find the hotel. The snow was an impenetrable wall of white, and he was unable to see more than a foot or two in front of him. He had heard of farmers who had frozen to death in blizzards because they'd gotten turned around and lost their way walking from cabin to barn. Before winter hit, most settlers strung guide ropes around their homestead, a lifeline they could hold on to when they had to venture outside to tend livestock.

But Matt had no lifeline. He was relying on instinct — that and feeling his way by keeping close to the buildings along the Front Street boardwalk, each slow, stumbling step a moment of danger and doubt. Every now and then he used his crutch to probe the thick white veil in front of him, wary of falling off the walk when it abruptly ended at one of Dodge's many alleys.

The big marshal was keenly aware that

making his way through the blizzard was a time to think like a man of action but act like a man of thought. The cold was cruel. Matt estimated the temperature had plunged to at least twenty below in the past hour, and every breath he took tasted like frosted ice crystals.

His left foot, covered only by a sock, was so numb he could no longer feel it, and his face was stiff, snow clinging to his eyebrows.

In the end, the lamps lit in the rooms at the Dodge House were dim beacons that helped guide him. Matt stomped into the lobby, nodded to the clerk and brushed snow off his coat.

"Not a day to be out walking, Marshal," the clerk chided. "Best to stay indoors."

The man obviously didn't know about the return of the bank robbers, and Matt decided now was not the time to enlighten him.

Stretching high above him were the stairs, as great a barrier going up as they had been coming down. Matt had thought to avoid those stairs as much as possible, but the events of the morning had now made that impossible.

He had to talk to Festus, and to do that, he had to hazard the stairs. There was no other way.

By the time he reached the landing, Matt was sweating heavily and his broken leg throbbed. He stepped along the corridor to Festus' room, his crutch thumping, and knuckled the door.

"Come on in," the deputy hollered. "It's open."

Matt opened the door and stomped inside. Festus was in bed, dressed in a nightshirt, his battered hat on his head. He was leafing through a picture book someone had brought him, and he looked up in surprise when the marshal entered.

"Matthew, what are you doing out of bed?" he asked. "You should be resting that broke leg."

Ignoring his deputy's question, Matt got right to the point. "Festus," he said, "I need your help."

Festus saw something in the marshal's face that disturbed him and he asked: "What's happened, Matthew?"

"Plenty," Matt answered. And he told him.

After the marshal stopped speaking, it took Festus long moments to think the situation through. Then he raised his left hand, scratched his hairy cheek and asked: "What do you have in mind, Matthew?"

"We have to get Kitty out of the Long

Branch, and we have to do it soon."

"We?"

Matt nodded. "Like I said, Festus, I need your help. You and me, we have to take back this town."

The deputy looked stricken. He nodded toward his right arm, bound up in a sling hanging from his neck. "Matthew, my gun hand is useless. What kind of help would I be?"

But the marshal was relentless. "If it comes down to shooting, you can hold the Greener in your left." Then, in a softer tone, he added: "Festus, I can't do this alone. I need you with me."

Festus shook his head, his eyes haunted. "How many of them bandits are there?" he asked.

"Far as I could tell, seven." Matt hesitated, wondering how his deputy would take the news. "Deacon Waters is one of them."

Shock showed on Festus' face. "The same Deacon Waters that gunned Dutchy Long down Las Cruces way a spell back?"

"In the flesh," Matt said. "And I'd say as rattlesnake dangerous as ever was."

Festus swallowed hard, like a man trying to force down a dry chicken bone. "Matthew, I knowed Dutchy Long. He was gun slick as they come, an' he'd killed maybe four or five named men. Hell, look at us, you with a broke leg an' me with a broke shoulder an' arm. Atween us both we don't even add up to a deputy deputy marshal."

Matt smiled. "You're right about that, but a couple of cripples or no, we got to do it."

"Do you have a plan, Matthew?" Festus asked, hope lighting in his eyes. "Something real smart like you always come up with?"

"Not this time, at least I don't have much of one," Matt admitted. "But, such as it is, my plan begins with getting Kitty to go to her room upstairs at the Long Branch."

"How we gonna do that?" Festus asked, one eyebrow crawling up his forehead like a hairy black caterpillar.

After Matt told him, Festus' face paled. "It's thin, Matthew, mighty thin. An' maybe Doc won't go fer it."

"That's a chance we'll have to take," Matt said.

Festus thought things through again, then said: "You'll have to help me into my pants an' sich, Matthew. Gettin' dressed is a reg'lar chore for a one-armed, shot-up deputy."

* * *

When Matt and Festus stepped out of the hotel, the wind took the empty sleeve of the deputy's ragged mackinaw and tossed it around wildly. Matt caught the flapping sleeve and tucked it into the pocket of the coat.

"How we even gonna make our way to Doc's place in this storm?" Festus asked, fat flakes of snow peppering his face. "It's clear to the other side of town."

"We'll do like I did, walk along the boardwalk and stay close to the buildings," Matt answered. "It isn't easy, but we can make it."

"If you say so, Matthew," Festus said, shivering, his face clouded by doubt. "But it's sure going to be a chore, an' no mistake."

Matt realized that his deputy was still very weak from his wounds and loss of blood. His face was ashen gray under his tan and his eyes were still bright with fever. But if Matt had any chance of defeating Scar Henry and saving Kitty and the others, he needed Festus. He needed the other man's courage and obstinate determination. Under the circumstances, half a Festus was better than no Festus at all.

It was about two in the afternoon as the

lawmen made their way back along the boardwalk toward Doc Adams' office. The snow had eased off slightly, though it lay two feet thick on the flat and drifts as high as a tall man were piling up against the sides of the buildings. The light had changed, the darkness giving way to a dull mother-of-pearl glow, and the wind was no longer gusting as truculently, though every now and then it blew hard.

But it was still bitterly cold, the air sharp and cutting, razor-edged and merciless.

The walking Matt had done had taken its toll on his broken leg; from knee to ankle, it pulsed with pain. A strip of tape holding the splints had worked loose and trailed two feet behind him.

Beside him, Festus staggered now and then as a random blast of wind hit him, and his breath was coming in short, labored gasps from his open mouth.

Matt felt a pang of guilt. His deputy was not a well man. He should be lying in bed right now, not bracing a blizzard and facing the looming likelihood of a gunfight against impossible odds.

Heads bent, the two lawmen worked their slow, painful way along the boardwalk, made slippery and treacherous by snow and under that a thin layer of ice.

Matt took ahold of Festus' good arm and helped him all he could, but every now and then the deputy had to stop and rest, fighting for the breath that came hard to him. But when he reached the marshal's office, Festus stepped inside the open door and took down the Greener from the rack.

"How you holding up, Festus?" Matt asked, his concern for the wounded man growing.

The deputy shrugged. "I'd have to be dead three days to start feelin' better, Matthew. But I reckon I'll stick."

"I knew you would," Matt said, meaning every word.

When Matt and Festus left the office, the snow had thinned out enough that they could see across the street to the Long Branch. A tall, lanky man, made bulky in a bearskin coat, was standing outside smoking a cigar. When he caught sight of the lawmen, he threw the cigar stub into the street and ducked inside.

A few moments later Scar Henry and Deacon Waters stepped onto the boardwalk. The two outlaws watched as Matt and Festus made their slow way toward Doc Adams's office. Finally Henry turned and said something to Waters. Then both men laughed, shook their heads, and went back into the saloon.

"What you reckon them two was sayin' about us, Matthew?" Festus asked, looking back at the Long Branch over his shoulder.

Matt's smile was as bitter as the cold itself. "I'd guess it was something about a couple of sorry cripples posing as lawmen," he said.

"They ain't even a stingy bit skeered of us, are they?"

The marshal shook his head. "No, they're not, Festus. But that might just work to our advantage."

Chapter 7

Doc Takes a Hand

A healthy man could have walked from the Dodge House to Doc Adams' home and surgery in less than three minutes. It took Matt and Festus three times that long and both men were exhausted by the time Matt banged on the physician's door.

After a few moments they heard Doc's irritated voice yell from inside. "I'm coming, damn it all! No need to knock the door down."

The door swung open, and Doc, a scowl on his face and a thick book in his hand, said: "Oh, it's you two. You should both be in bed."

"Can we come in, Doc?" Matt asked. "It's real important."

Doc stood aside and ushered the two lawmen into his hallway. He glanced down at Matt's unraveling splints and growled: "You have to stay off that leg for a while. If you don't it won't heal."

"Maybe later, Doc," Matt said as he followed Doc into his comfortable, warm parlor. "Right now we have us a problem."

Doc sighed, carefully closed his book and laid it on the table. "What can I do for you?" he asked.

The big marshal glanced at the book cover: *Essays and Observations on Natural History, Anatomy and Physiology.*

Doc followed Matt's eyes and said: "That was written by Dr. John Hunter, a fine surgeon. I just wish I was half as good."

"But you are real good, Doc," Festus said, making an effort to reassure the man. "Jes' lookit how many bullets you've cut out o' folks, to say nothin' of arrowheads an' sich."

"Thank you, Deputy Haggen," Doc said, making a wry face. "Your confidence in my medical abilities touches me to the quick."

"Think nothing of it, Doc." Festus grinned, the physician's sarcasm winging right over his head.

"We need those medical abilities over to the Long Branch, Doc," Matt said quickly. "There are two wounded men inside." He hesitated for a heartbeat, then added: "And one dead man."

Doc stiffened. "What happened?"

As he had done earlier for Festus, in as

few words as possible, Matt told Doc about the return of the outlaws, the threats against Kitty and the other hostages and the murder of Chet Lagrange.

"I'll get over there right away," Doc said after he'd heard Matt through. "How badly hurt are those men?"

Matt shrugged. "I don't know, Doc. Things were happening pretty fast when I was there."

"Come into the surgery, Matt," the physician said. "Before I go, I've got to rebind the splints on your leg." He turned to Festus. "And I'll take a look at those wounds of yours."

"Before you do all that, Doc," Matt said. "I want to ask you to do something for me when you get to the saloon."

It had been many years since Matt Dillon had punched cows, but by force of long habit, he still carried a tally book and a stub of pencil. He wrote on a page of the book, then tore it off and handed it to Doc. The physician quickly scanned the note:

COME DARK GO TO YOUR ROOM.
GO TO THE WINDOW.

"Well, at least it's spelled correctly," Doc said. "What do I do with this?"

"Give it to Kitty," Matt said. "Without being seen."

Doc nodded, aware of the urgency in Matt's voice. "I'll see what I can do."

The big marshal's face was suddenly troubled. "Doc, there's one more thing. I believe Scar Henry will keep you there. The town's only doctor is a mighty valuable hostage."

"Thought of that already," Doc said. "But there are wounded men over there who need my help. I guess that's a chance I'll just have to take."

A few minutes later Matt and Festus watched Doc, medical bag in hand, angle across Front Street and step into the Long Branch.

"Now what, Matthew?" Festus asked.

"Festus, now we wait for nightfall. In the meantime we'll spread the word of what's happened and tell folks to stay well clear of the Long Branch," Matt said. He looked intently at his deputy, trying to gauge his reserves of strength. "Can you make it across the tracks and let people over there know what's going on?"

Without hesitation, Festus nodded. "Sure I can. You heard what Doc said about my shoulder an' arm, Matthew. No sign of infection, he said." Festus smiled, pleased. "Yup, that's what he said all right."

Matt's smile matched that of his deputy's. "Then go to it, old-timer. And step right careful."

After the lawmen split up, Matt stomped carefully along the icy boardwalk toward his office. The snow had lessened even more and the wind had dropped, making only a low sound as it tossed a few fluttering flakes along Front Street. For the time being at least, the blizzard had blown itself out, though Matt calculated it had dumped at least twenty-four inches of snow on Dodge in the past three hours. It was bitterly cold and his breath smoked as he passed the Alhambra. Two men standing on the boardwalk outside the saloon were deeply engaged in conversation, a sight that gave Matt pause.

One of the two was the gambler and sometime pimp Earl Bodine and the man with him was his faithful shadow, Cole Fleming, a hulking giant and overbearing bully with shoulder-length hair and a dull, brutal face.

Despite the cold, Bodine wore only his gambler's finery, an expensively cut gray frockcoat, boiled white shirt and brocaded vest, an elegant contrast to Fleming's filthy, matted buffalo coat, drawn together at the waist with rope.

Earl Bodine was a troublemaker, a drifting cardsharp who had stayed on after the cowboys left to shack up with one of the Alhambra's resident whores. He had a vague reputation as a gunman and was said to have killed three men. Fleming had just been released after serving eight years in the Wyoming Territorial Prison for murder; he'd followed the herds into Dodge early last spring. He and Bodine, kindred spirits, had hit it off right away and the pair had been inseparable ever since.

Matt had some suspicion that the two had rolled drunk cowboys and had been involved in the murder of Ella Campbell, a young prostitute who'd been found knifed to death in her crib behind the Alamo Saloon.

The marshal had never been able to find enough evidence to arrest Bodine and Fleming, a failure that still rankled him.

When Bodine glanced across the street and saw Matt looking at him, the gambler's eyes dropped guiltily. But Fleming gave the marshal a belligerent, challenging stare, as though daring him to say something.

Matt let it go. It was not a crime for a

couple of men to have a conversation in the street, even tinhorns like those two.

But what were they plotting?

The big marshal shook his head and stumped on to his office. Right now he had problems enough without worrying about Earl Bodine.

Before long, Festus arrived back at the marshal's office. "I done like you tole me, Matthew," the deputy said. "But the word already got around. Seems like ol' Scar is a right sociable feller and is giving out free drinks to everybody who steps inside the Long Branch. Only thing is, he's been making right sure to warn folks that if they try to stop him clearing out the other banks, he'll kill all his prisoners."

"You mean he's letting men come and go?"

Festus nodded, pouring himself a cup of coffee. "He surely is, except for them posse men an' Sam Noonan an' Miss Kitty."

"And now they've got Doc," Matt said, his words as bitter as the coffee in his deputy's cup.

"He hasn't come out yet?" Festus asked.

Matt shook his head. "I reckon Henry is keeping him, just like I feared."

The office door swung open and Mayor James Kelley and several townsmen stomped inside, a gust of windblown snow flurrying around them.

Without any preamble, Kelley got down to brass tacks. "Matt, these men have been telling me what's happening over to the Long Branch, and it scares the bejabbers out of me." Kelley frowned, stabbing a finger at the marshal. "What do you intend to do about it?"

Matt opened his mouth to speak, but Kelley never gave him the chance. "Here's what we do — we storm the place with a body of good men, arrest the bandits and free those prisoners." He nodded to the men around him, seeking their encouragement. "That's what we do."

"And then you'll count your dead, Mayor," Matt said, anger flaring in him. "Scar Henry's reservation in hell was made the day he was born, so he won't hesitate to kill Kitty and the others. I already watched him shoot down Chet Lagrange. Afterward Scar smiled, like he'd just stepped on a bug."

The mayor hesitated for a few moments, frowning in thought. Then his face cleared. "We charge them, Matt. We'll assault the saloon so fast, from front and back, that them bandits won't have time to kill anybody."

Matt shook his head, his exasperation growing. "Don't you think they're expecting a play like that?" He stomped closer to Kelley. "Listen, Mayor. Scar Henry is a killer and he's a skilled gunman. But worse, he has a man named Deacon Waters with him. Waters is fast, maybe the fastest there is or ever was. I heard that even John Wesley Hardin was careful to step around him. With Henry and Waters there, try to charge the Long Branch and I guarantee Percy Crump will be busy making coffins for a dozen dead citizens."

The men clustered around the mayor stirred and exchanged uncomfortable glances. These men were not weaklings and cowards — the West had a way of weeding out that kind — but they were all married with families, and Matt saw that they didn't relish the thought of bucking the odds by going up against a pair of skilled professional gunmen.

Even Mayor Kelley saw the light. Suddenly looking old, he said: "Jesus, Mary and Joseph and all the saints in Heaven help us. What are we going to do, Matt?"

"For now, we sit tight," Matt said. He looked the mayor in the eye. "I'll find a way."

"You'd better," Kelley said, drawing

what was left of his bluster around him like a ragged cloak. "Or Dodge City will be looking for a new marshal."

While Matt had been talking to the mayor, he'd been keeping a wary eye on the gathering dusk. Now it was time to put his rescue plan into operation.

But had Doc managed to pass his note to Kitty? The marshal could only hope the physician had found a way.

"You ready, Festus?" Matt asked.

The deputy looked tired beyond tired. His face was ashen and there were deep, dark circles under his eyes. But Festus Haggen had sand and he showed it now. He picked up the Greener and managed a grin. "I'll be all right. Let's go rescue the fair maiden in distress."

Matt was taken aback. "How come you know about fair maidens in distress?" he asked.

Festus' grin widened, then grew shy. "One of my lady friends read that to me out of a picture book she brung me. It was all about fair maidens an' dragons an' gallant knights ridin' to the rescue." The deputy shrugged his good shoulder. "I guess that's what we are, Matthew, gallant knights a-ridin' to the rescue."

"In mighty rusty armor," Matt said, leaning his weight on his good leg. He waved a hand toward the door and bowed. "Lead on, Sir Galahad."

The two lawmen stepped out into the snow-flecked darkness. A few lamps had been lit along Front Street, their flames guttering in the wind, splashing dancing circles of yellow-and-orange light on the slushy boardwalks.

It was very cold, a numbing freeze that had transformed Dodge into a crystalline town of frost and snow. Icicles hung from the eaves of the buildings, and when the wind gusted, brief veils of white lifted from the tops of the drifts.

A piano played at the Long Branch, and as Matt and Festus began to cross the street, they heard a man's coarse laugh, soon joined by another.

Staying wide of the saloon, the two lawmen struggled through the couple of feet of snow blanketing the street, then reached a wide alley that separated the Long Branch from the New York Hat Shop.

There was no moon, but the snow gleamed with its own light, illuminating a dim path through the bottle-strewn passageway.

Once behind the hat store, Matt and Festus rested a few moments. Away from the streetlights, the night was as dark as the bottom of a dry well, but Matt could make out the inverted V of the high drift that had piled up against the back of the Long Branch. Kitty's room was on the second floor. If Doc had managed to pass her the note, she would not have far to jump. The peak of the drift was only about six feet from the window ledge.

Matt in the lead, he and Festus stepped to the rear of the saloon. A beer delivery wagon, its tongue raised, was covered in snow to the top of its huge steel-rimmed wheels. Out in the white wilderness of the prairie, hungry coyotes were calling, moving like gray ghosts through a wintry wind that carried with it the smell of distant mountains.

A narrow pathway from the back door of the Long Branch to the outhouse had been cleared of snow, and seeing this, Matt felt a momentary pang of alarm. If one of the robbers stepped through that door, he would have to shoot. Then the ball would open — and the lives of Kitty and the imprisoned men inside would not be worth a plug nickel.

Matt moved to the wagon, struggling

through a deep drift. Festus, his shotgun up and ready in his left hand, followed, his eyes on Kitty's window. Her room was in darkness, frost lacing the glass panes.

Festus, in a low, urgent whisper, voiced Matt's unspoken fear. "Matthew, what if one o' them bandits decides to step out back?"

"If he spots us, cut loose with the Greener," Matt said. "Then I'll do my best to rush inside and try to nail Henry and Waters."

The deputy let out a low whistle. "I sure hope it don't come to that, Matthew. With you on a crutch an' all, I figure you'd be buckin' a losin' game."

Matt nodded. "I would, no question about that. Let's just hope the freeze is enough to keep Henry and his men inside." The big marshal looked up at the building. "Come on, Kitty," he whispered urgently. "Come to the window."

A few more minutes ticked by. Flurries of snow swirled around the two lawmen and Matt was so numb from cold, he could not feel his feet or hands. Festus was hunched into the upturned collar of his mackinaw, frost clinging to his bearded cheeks.

Matt stuck his gun hand in his coat pocket and worked his fingers, trying to bring back some feeling. Beside him Festus shivered and was no longer able to control the chattering of his teeth. The deputy's hand clutched around the stock of the Greener had turned pure white, blue veins showing.

Another five minutes passed, then five more.

Matt was worried. If Kitty did not appear soon, he and Festus could freeze to death out there. And if they were seen, both of them would be too stiff to move and defend themselves.

A lamp flared in Kitty's room.

A sudden rectangle of yellow light was cast on the flat snow around Matt's feet and a shadow moved across the window.

As Matt watched, Kitty came to the window and looked outside. The big marshal struggled his way further into the light and waved. Kitty waved back.

The woman glanced over her shoulder, then tried to push the window open, failed and tried again. It was frozen solid and would not budge.

Looking down at Matt, Kitty shrugged helplessly. The marshal, his heart hammering, motioned to her to try again. It was no use. The window was frosted shut.

Beside him, Matt was aware of Festus

looking fearfully at the back door. The deputy held his shotgun like a pistol in one hand, barrels pointed at the doorway.

There was only one thing for it — Kitty would have to smash the window and pray that no one heard her.

Matt tucked his crutch under his arm and made a sweeping motion with both hands, mimicking a man swinging a chair. Did she get it?

Kitty understood, but she waved away Matt's suggestion. She turned and disappeared into the room. When she came back, she had a bottle of whiskey in her hand.

Quickly, Kitty poured whiskey around the window frame until the bottle was empty, then readied herself to try again.

Festus touched his tongue to his top lip and whispered: "Kitty always has the best an' I just bet that was bonded Kentucky bourbon." He shook his head. "Pity."

Kitty tried the window again — and this time it budged an inch. She got her fingers under the window and heaved upward. The window slid open a foot, then another. It was enough. She turned away and a few moments later a carpetbag sailed through the open window. Then Kitty, headfirst, wriggled through after it.

She cleared the window and hit the ice-covered drift, slid a few feet, then vanished from sight, completely swallowed by the rampart of snow.

Matt hobbled to the drift, leaned over and began to push the snow aside. Kitty's head appeared, then her shoulders. She freed a hand and held it up. Matt took the woman's hand, hauled, and Kitty came clear, her hair, wool dress and cloak covered in a dusting of white.

"Let's go," Matt whispered, casting an urgent glance at the open window.

Kitty picked up her carpetbag. "Where?" she asked.

"My office," Matt said, taking her arm. "You'll be safe there."

Kitty's face was a white oval in the darkness. "Matt," she said, "he'll come looking for me."

"Scar Henry won't find you, Kitty," Matt said, holding the woman close. "And if he does, he'll have to step over my dead body to get to you."

Chapter 8

A Gambler Cashes In His Chips

When the two lawmen and Kitty returned to the office, Matt closed the door and slammed the iron bolt in place. He drew over the heavy pine shutters on both windows, each cut with a slit for a rifleman. Then he and Festus laid the loaded Winchester and Henry on the table along with the extra boxes of ammunition. Matt reckoned he and his deputy were now as ready as they would ever be. The next move was up to the outlaws.

The railroad clock on the office wall stood at six when there was a commotion outside, a pounding of booted feet on the boardwalk and the shouts and curses of angry men.

"I guess Scar Henry discovered you're missing, Kitty," Matt said.

Kitty's beautiful face was white-lipped and her eyes were wild, tangled with fright. "He's not a man, Matt. He's some kind of wild animal. After Doc passed me your note, I told Henry I had to go upstairs and freshen my makeup. He said to stay there because he'd be up soon." Kitty shuddered. "Matt, he told me what he was going to do to me. Vile things. Terrible things. He told me he'd use me hard, and when he was finished, he'd throw what was left of me to his men."

Kitty's face drained of color. "I was so afraid, Matt. He's . . . he's . . ."

Matt stomped across the floor and took Kitty in his arms. "No one is going to hurt you," he whispered. "I won't let them. You're safe here."

"That's right," Festus said, concern battling anger in his eyes. "That low-down skunk ain't gonna get past me and Matthew, Miss Kitty, an' that's a natural fact."

Kitty gave Festus a grateful smile, then gasped and clutched at Matt when Henry's voice yelled from outside.

"You, in the jail!"

"What do you want?" Festus shouted back.

"I want my woman. Send her out now."

Matt released Kitty from his arms, picked up the Winchester and thumped to the door. "Scar!" he shouted. "You want her, come and get her."

"Damn you, Dillon!" Henry yelled. "I told you what would happen if you interfered with me. Now you're gonna see my bona fides."

A couple of slow minutes ticked past. Then from the window gun slit, Matt saw Henry and a couple of his men drag one of the wounded posse members into the street.

"Dillon!" Henry yelled. "Send out my woman, or by God, I'll kill this man."

Matt shoved his rifle through the gun slit and took careful aim. "And a split second afterward, I'll drop you, Scar," he called out.

Henry was caught flat-footed and he knew it. Driven by anger and lust, he'd left himself wide-open, an easy target against the white backdrop of the snow.

Henry backed up a few steps and yelled over his shoulder: "Deke, can you hear me?"

"I hear you, Dave," the gunman answered.

"If Dillon shoots me, kill all the prisoners, including that damned pill roller."

"Depend on it, Dave," Waters yelled, a laugh in his voice. "I'll gun the doc first."

Henry took a step back, then another. He put up his arms, his palms facing Matt. "Don't you go shooting me, Dillon," he yelled. "No need to go shooting me."

The outlaw took another backward step, then another. Matt held his fire. Suddenly Henry turned, sprinted toward the door of the Long Branch, then crashed his way through.

Out on the street, the prisoner, a man Matt recognized as Micah Jones, one of Percy Crump's assistants, looked quickly around him. Unable to believe his luck, he stepped toward the marshal's office, a bandaged leg dragging.

"Marshal Dillon!" he hollered. "Let me in!"

Matt unbolted the door. Jones was almost at the boardwalk when a rifle's flat statement hammered from just inside the Long Branch.

Hit hard, Jones screamed and fell face-first in the snow. He tried to rise, but a second bullet slammed into him and this time he lay still.

"Damn you, Dillon!" Henry yelled from across the street. "That's not the end of it. There will be a heap more dead men afore this is over."

Matt swung his sights on the saloon door. His finger took up the slack on the trigger and he held his breath. He stood that way for long moments, then the breath hissed out of him and he took the Winchester from his shoulder. A shot from him and more innocent men would die inside the saloon, maybe all of them. As badly as he wanted to kill Henry, he could not take that chance.

A helpless anger riding him, Matt cursed and threw the rifle on the table. "Henry is right. Before this is over, there will be more dead men," he said. "But I swear to God, he'll be one of them."

As the long night crept by on cat feet, Kitty slept on Matt's cot, and he and Festus took turns on guard. Matt was exhausted, plunging into a dreamless sleep as soon as his head hit the lumpy mattress in one of the cells behind the office.

Each time Festus wakened him to take his turn at the window, it seemed he'd only been asleep for a couple of minutes, not the two-hour duration of the other man's watch.

When dawn finally touched the edges of the sullen snow clouds with tarnished bronze, Matt stumped from his post at the window, fed wood into the stove and put coffee on to boil.

He was bone tired and his leg ached, but the sight of Kitty asleep, long lashes fanning over high cheekbones, the small sound of her breathing a soft song in the room, cheered him and he drew strength from her presence.

When the coffee began to bubble in the pot, he stepped to the window again and looked outside.

An uncertain gray light was washing away the blue shadows from the miniature ridges and mesas the wind had carved into the snowdrifts, but the false fronts of the buildings across the street were still rectangular silhouettes of darkness against the lesser dark of the sky.

It was not yet eight, but lamps were being lit in the stores and businesses along Front Street and drippy-nosed clerks in plug hats and long woolen mufflers were already on their way to work, carefully tramping along the icy boardwalks.

"Anthin' stirrin' at the Long Branch, Matthew?" Festus asked, stepping to Matt's elbow, sleep still heavy in his eyes.

The marshal shook his head. "Not a thing. But I'm sure Scar Henry has his guards posted."

Festus poured coffee for himself and Matt, then motioned with an empty cup. "How about Miss Kitty?" he asked.

"Let her sleep," Matt answered. "She had a rough day yesterday."

Kitty woke an hour later, as a light snow again began to fall on Dodge. Matt brought her coffee, then carried a chair beside the cot. They sat in a comfortable silence, sipping from steaming cups, two people completely at ease with each other, knowing no words were needed.

A few minutes later, as Festus refilled their cups, feet pounded on the boardwalk outside and someone hammered on the door. "What is it?" Matt yelled, fearing a trap.

"Bodkin's bank is being robbed, Marshal!" a man's voice called out, loud and urgent. "They're getting away!"

Scar Henry!

Matt rose, grabbed his crutch and buckled on his gun belt. Festus took up the Greener and the two lawmen hurried to the door and stepped outside.

The three robbers were already urging their floundering horses along the street, snow lifting in high white bursts from flailing hooves.

But it wasn't Scar Henry and his men.

Earl Bodine in a long gray coat, red muffler and stovepipe hat was in the lead. Just behind him rode Cole Fleming and then a young girl in a black cloak, the hood pulled up over her blond curls, sacks of money draped over the front of her saddle. Both Bodine and Fleming had guns in their hands.

But the commotion caused by the robbery of the bank had not gone unnoticed by Henry.

Ahead of Bodine and Fleming stood one man, arms folded across his chest, a slight bemused smile on his lips.

On the boardwalk outside the Long Branch, Scar Henry watched, Doc Adams in front of him as a human shield.

Straddle-legged, Deacon Waters waited in the middle of the street until Bodine was six or seven yards from him.

From the boardwalk, Matt yelled: "Waters! No!"

What came next happened so fast, the marshal had no chance to intervene.

Waters drew. He pulled both his guns with blurring, unbelievable speed, two hammers coming back at the same time, two shots sounding as one.

Bodine was hit. He reeled in the saddle and yanked his horse to his right. Fleming, also hit, took the bullet without visible effect. The man reined his mount to a stop, threw a curse at Waters and raised his Colt to eye level. Waters fired again from both his Smith & Wessons. A sudden red rose blossomed between Bodine's eyes and the gambler screamed and fell into the snow. Fleming fired and a spiteful V of white kicked up at Waters' feet. Waters shot again and this time Fleming was hit high in the chest. The man tried to raise his gun, but all at once it seemed too heavy for him. His mouth wide-open in a silent, angry bellow at the manner of his dying, Fleming slid from the saddle and hit the ground, a brief explosion of snow erupting around his huge body.

The girl, her face twisted in fear, pulled her horse around, desperately trying to escape. Waters' guns barked and the girl tumbled over her horse's head, hit the snow and lay still.

As the hammering echoes of Waters' guns faded, Matt drew his Colt and yelled: "Waters! Drop your guns!"

"No arrests, Dillon!" Henry called from across the street. "Deke keeps his guns or I'll blow this medicine man's head clean off his shoulders."

"Matt!" Doc hollered. "Forget about me! Arrest that damned killer!"

The triple click of the hammer as Henry's gun came to full cock was loud in the silence. He pushed the muzzle hard into Doc's temple. "Your call, Dillon," he said. "Back off or I scatter this man's brains."

"Marshal, you won't be taking my guns anyhow, not today or any other day," Waters said, turning to face Matt, the smoking Smiths hanging relaxed at his sides. His smile was thin, without humor. "But, like Dave says, it's your call."

Matt felt trapped, but under the circumstances there was only one thing he could do. "Henry," he yelled, "I won't sacrifice the life of a good man for murdering trash like you and Waters. Let him go."

"Thought you might see it that way." Henry grinned. He took his gun away from Doc's head, but held the outraged physician at arm's length. "But I ain't letting him go."

Henry walked away from the door of the saloon, dragging Doc with him, snow swirling around both men. The outlaw stepped to the edge of the boardwalk and spread his hands wide, an expansive gesture that took in the groups of gaping people clustered around watching him.

"That man," Henry yelled, pointing at Bodine's sprawled body, "tried to take what was mine. That's why I done for him. Let this be a lesson to all of you. Dave Henry keeps what's his'n, his money" —

he looked directly at Matt — "and his woman."

"That's telling them, Dave," Waters said, his humorless grin oddly dismissive, like Henry was spouting the same hot air he'd heard before. "Only it was me as done for him."

The gunman reloaded, then holstered his guns and high-stepped through the snow to the dead girl's horse. He took the moneybags from the saddle, glanced uninterestedly at the girl's body, then spent more time studying the already stiffening corpses of Bodine and Fleming.

Matt recognized Waters' interest as the cold postmortem examination of the professional gunman. He was checking the placement of his shots. He had dropped the girl with only one bullet, but she didn't count. However he had fired four rounds to kill two men and now he slowly shook his head, as though telling himself that next time he must do better.

And watching him, Matt felt a sudden chill. He had seen Waters draw and shoot . . . and he knew that on his best day he couldn't match that kind of flashing speed.

Chapter 9

Dire Tidings

It seemed to Matt that the only person prospering in Dodge that cold winter was Percy Crump. Like a vulture, the undertaker's business was death and recently business had been good.

After Crump had cleared the four bodies from Front Street, Kitty sat at Matt's desk while Festus stood guard at a window. The woman's face showed the strain of the past twenty-four hours and there was a wounded sadness in her eyes.

"The dead girl's name was Molly O'Rourke," she told Matt. "She left the Five Corners slum of New York a couple of years ago and came west hoping for a better life. She met Earl Bodine, saw his gold ring and fancy clothes and thought he could give it to her."

"How old was she?" Matt asked.

Kitty's shoulders shrugged in her gray woolen dress. "Seventeen, maybe younger."

Matt nodded. "All Bodine gave her was an early grave." His eyes angled in the direction of the street. "Him and Deacon Waters."

"I just don't understand why Earl Bodine robbed the bank," Kitty said. "I knew he was a five-ace tinhorn and gold-brick artist, but I never pegged him as a bank robber."

Matt's smile was grim. "Scar Henry showed him the way, so he figured it would be easy. He just didn't count on Waters."

"What's going to happen, Matt?" Kitty asked. "If I don't go back to Henry, will he kill Doc and the others?"

Matt would not lie to her. "I think he will. If not Doc, then somebody else."

Kitty shook her head. "Matt, I won't let someone die for me. I couldn't bear to live with that on my conscience."

The big marshal shifted his weight in the chair. Now he tried to ease Kitty's fears. "Maybe Henry will just ride out of here after the snow lets up." He shrugged.

"But you really don't think that will happen, do you?"

"No, Kitty, it won't, because I aim to stop him. I plan on seeing Scar Henry and Deacon Waters hang."

"How can you stop him, Matt? You and Festus are in no shape to take on Henry and his bunch of killers."

"We're stove up some, I admit," Matt said, smiling. "But we'll find a way."

"I don't know if you're being brave or just plain foolish," Kitty said. "Maybe it's a combination of both."

A smile again tugged at Matt's lips. "I don't know about being foolish, but maybe I am. As for bravery, that's just going out and doing what you're afraid to do. A man can't be brave unless he's scared." The marshal's smile widened. "And right now I know I'm borrowing trouble and that's making me plenty scared."

Kitty laid her slender fingers on the back of Matt's huge hand. "Matt, I've been around men all my life, all kinds of men. They came at me with different faces, saying different things, but I learned early to ignore the talk and read what was in their eyes." She leaned closer to Matt. "Right now I'm reading your eyes but I don't see fear."

Matt laughed. "Then what do you see?"

Kitty shrugged. "Anger, determination, maybe some pain. And I think Scar Henry is so arrogant he's yet to realize something."

"And what's that?"

"That Matt Dillon is brave — and a mighty dangerous enemy."

★ ★ ★

By noon, Scar Henry had made no move against the marshal's office, nor had he threatened to kill another of his prisoners.

The sky had cleared, showing wide expanses of blue between retreating white clouds, but the temperature still hovered around twenty below. The branches of the cottonwoods lining the banks of the Arkansas looked like glass under their layers of ice, and every window in Dodge was brocaded with frost.

The snow served to muffle sound and a deep silence lay over the town, broken only by the cries of the black crows fluttering over the rooftops in untidy flight, drawn by blood and the smell of death.

Shortly before one, Jed Owens, the banker, pounded on the door of the marshal's office and Matt let the man come inside. Owens was buttoned into a thick wool greatcoat. The yellow muffler wrapped twice around his neck was so long it almost trailed on the ground at his feet.

"I just thought you'd want to know about poor Jane Morgan, Marshal," Owens said, spreading his hands to the stove, talking over his shoulder.

"How is she?" Matt asked.

"Not good, not good at all." Owens

turned and faced the marshal. "She's grieving terribly for her husband, especially since she's with child again."

"Matt, do you want me to go to her?" Kitty asked. "I didn't know she was pregnant."

The marshal shook his head. "No, that would be too dangerous."

Owens understood the situation. "Don't worry, Miss Kitty. My missus will visit her later this afternoon, and Jane has other women with her right now. Unfortunately she got real upset at Percy Crump's bad news. He says Silas can't be buried until the ground softens up in the spring. From now until then, he'll have to keep him on ice" — the banker hesitated a moment — "along with the other . . . uh . . . recently deceased."

"Newly O'Brien has dynamite," Festus said. "Maybe he could blast holes in the ground."

"It's a possibility, I suppose," Owens said. "But I don't think the mayor would take kindly to Newly blowing up the town cemetery. Mr. Kelley seems to set store by the place."

The big banker was silent for a few moments, deep in thought, as though carefully considering his next words. Then he said: "Marshal, are any efforts being made to recover the bank's money from the robbers?" As though apologizing for such a materialistic question when so many were dying, Owens added quickly: "Not only will I be ruined, but so will most, if not all, of my depositors."

"I'll get your money back, Owens," Matt said, the skin around his eyes tightening. "I don't plan on letting Scar Henry ride out of Dodge."

The banker glanced at Matt's splinted leg and then to pale, hollow-eyed Festus and seemed to gather no confidence from what he saw. "If you need help, Marshal, you know you only have to call on me," he said, his offer of assistance a thinly disguised expression of doubt.

Matt nodded and smiled slightly. "I appreciate that, Owens."

Lost for more words, Owens opened his mouth to speak, closed it again then settled for: "Well, I'll bid you good day." He touched his hat brim and bowed slightly. "Miss Kitty." The banker matched Matt's smile with one that was even slighter, nodding in Kitty's direction. "One of my major depositors," he said.

After Owens left, the slow, stately ticking of the office clock tallied time until ten after two when a fist hammered on the door and a man yelled: "Marshal, it's John Quigley! Let me in! Dire tidings!"

Festus opened the door wide enough for Quigley to sidle inside before bolting it shut again.

Quigley, a small man with long, frizzy sideburns and the quick black eyes of a bird, was the ticket agent at the Santa Fe rail depot. He stepped to Matt's desk and words tumbled out of him. "Marshal, there's a train frozen to the tracks about ten miles down the line. Been there since yesterday. Fifteen, twenty people on board, maybe more."

"How do you know this, John?" Matt asked.

"The conductor, a man named Winfield, just made it to the depot. He took off for help on snowshoes and right now I'd say he's mighty near froze to death his ownself."

Quigley took off his round cap and ran nervous fingers through his thinning hair. "Winfield says the rescue trains are still miles away because they can't buck through the drifts farther down the line. It could be a week, maybe two, before they get through."

Pressing home the urgency of the crisis, Quigley pointed dramatically to the west.

"Winfield says the wood for the stoves in the cars is about all gone and them passengers could freeze to death if they don't get help real soon."

Matt nodded, his mind made up. "I'll talk to the mayor about organizing a rescue party," he said. He rose to his feet and grabbed his crutch. "Festus, do you think you could ask his honor if he'd grace us with his presence?"

Festus smiled from his post at the window. "I'll go get him. Jes' keep an eye on the Long Branch, Matthew. I sure don't trust that snake Scar Henry."

After Festus left, cradling the Greener, Quigley said: "Marshal, Winfield told me that one of them passengers is Isobel Charles-Greenwood. She was on her way to join her husband, a cavalry officer at Fort Dodge."

Quigley obviously expected the name to register with Matt and the agent's face dropped in disappointment when the marshal asked: "I should know her?"

"Know her? I should say!" Quigley exclaimed, shocked at Matt's ignorance. "She's only the daughter of Barton Charles, one of the ten richest men in the world. Made his money as an arms manufacturer during the War Between the

States, and since then he's branched into railroads, mining and shipping and a heap of other ventures besides."

Matt grinned. "Then I guarantee Mayor Kelley will redouble his efforts to rescue the young lady. He seems to set store by rich folks."

A few minutes later Mayor Kelley, still smarting at Matt for turning down his plan to storm the Long Branch, barged into the office, the icy air blasting inside with him no less frigid than his demeanor.

"All right, Marshal," he demanded, "what's all this I'm hearing from Festus about frozen trains and frozen people?"

Matt recounted Quigley's story to Kelley, and when he'd finished, he added: "And one of the passengers is apparently a very important person, a rich heiress." He turned to the agent. "What's that gal's double-barreled name again?"

"Mrs. Isobel Charles-Greenwood," Quigley supplied, obviously irritated that Matt had forgotten it so quickly.

Kelley's eyebrows climbed up his forehead. "Mmm . . . odd name . . . and rich." He stroked his chin, thinking. "She wouldn't be any relation to the famous Barton Charles, would she? A niece maybe?"

"His daughter," Quigley answered.

"Ah, then this rescue becomes a matter of supreme urgency," Kelley said.

"Under the circumstances I will, of course, lead the rescue party myself."

"Can horses get through to the train, John?" Matt asked. "And a couple of wagons maybe?"

The agent nodded. "Uh-huh. Part of the way at least. Winfield says there are deep drifts across the tracks and other places, but on the flat the snow is only a couple of feet deep and it's frosted hard. I reckon the wagons could get pretty close and maybe make it all the way."

Kelley clapped his hands together. "Then horses and wagons it is. I'll round up the volunteers right away." He looked at Matt and inclined his head in the direction of the Long Branch. "Have you come up with a plan yet?" he asked.

"I'm working on it, Mayor," Matt replied.

"See you do," Kelley said shortly. "I don't plan on allowing this standoff to go on much longer." He found a cigar in his pocket and thumbed a match into flame. "If the weather holds, Henry and the rest will pull out soon," he said from behind a cloud of blue smoke. "I don't want them leaving with the town's money."

"I won't let that happen, Mayor," Matt said, his voice flat, offering no chance for argument.

Kelley's gaze locked on the marshal, and he found himself looking into gunmetal blue eyes that had suddenly shaded hard and were colder than any he'd ever seen. The mayor stiffened, realizing that many a hard case had carried the sight of those eyes to the grave.

"I don't believe you will, Marshal," Kelley said, shaken, feeling icy fingers run up and down his back. "I don't believe you will let it happen."

"You count on it, Mayor," Matt said.

Matt stepped to the window and watched Kelley leave. Quigley stood uncertainly on the boardwalk for a few moments, looking over to the Long Branch. He rubbed his fingers across his mouth, made up his mind about something, and quickly crossed the street before disappearing into the saloon.

Matt could do nothing to stop the agent. He could only hope that Quigley, a talkative man, would not blab about a rich heiress named Isobel Charles-Greenwood isolated and vulnerable on a stalled train.

Scar Henry would be mighty interested.

Chapter 10

Matt Strikes Back

Just before two in the afternoon, Mayor Kelley assembled a couple of freight wagons he and a dozen volunteers had loaded with food and blankets. The wagons would later be used to haul the train passengers back to Dodge.

Kelley rode down Front Street at the head of his rescue party, and to Matt's annoyance, the fact that Mrs. Isobel Charles-Greenwood was on the frozen train seemed to be one of the worst-kept secrets in Dodge.

Townspeople stood on the boardwalks and cheered as the mayor rode past, prompting Festus to note that Kelley was the only man he knew who could strut while sitting a saddle.

Ten minutes later, four of Henry's gunmen left the Long Branch and headed in the direction of the livery stable. Matt watched the outlaws ride in the tracks of the wagons, rifles booted under their knees.

John Quigley, a talkative man, had blabbed and soon the whole town had known about the rich young heiress.

And the alert Scar Henry had seen a golden opportunity. The money from the Dodge banks was chicken feed compared to the king's ransom he could extort from Barton Charles for the safe return of his daughter.

That girl was worth ten, twenty, a hundred times more than her weight in gold, and a man could do plenty with that kind of money.

Deep in thought, Matt realized then that Henry was down to just two men: Deacon Waters and one other.

If he was going to make his move, now was the time. The question was how to strike at Henry without endangering the lives of Doc and the other men in the saloon.

Maybe a direct assault on the Long Branch wasn't the way.

The big marshal looked down at his splinted leg. Could he ride? If he went after the four gunmen who were following the mayor, he might be able to cut down the odds and ensure the safety of Mrs. Isobel What's-her-name at the same time.

It was not in Matt Dillon's nature to

allow himself to be pushed, and so far it had been Scar Henry and his gang who'd done all the pushing. It was high time to start evening the score. Matt came to a decision. He would stop those riders and frustrate Henry's plan to kidnap the woman.

The marshal stumped on his crutch to the table and picked up his Winchester.

"Matt," Kitty said, alarm flaring in her eyes, "what are you going to do?"

"Scar Henry just sent four of his boys out of town, and I reckon they're going after that Greenwood gal," he answered. "I plan on stopping them."

Kitty rose to her feet. "You can't do that. You can't ride with a broken leg."

"I'm surely about to try," Matt said. "Scar Henry has left me pretty low, Kitty. The good news is that I've no further to fall. Now it's time to stop being a cripple and start being a lawman again."

Kitty turned on Festus, a helpless anger staining scarlet on her cheeks. "Festus, you talk some sense into him. It seems I can't."

The deputy scratched his cheek, hunting words. Finally he said: "Matthew, let me come with you."

Matt shook his head. "You're in no shape to ride, Festus. Besides, I need you and your shotgun here. Scar Henry might decide to attack the office."

"Festus, you're as bad as Matt!" Kitty yelled. "Now do what I told you and talk him out of it."

"Can't, Miss Kitty," the deputy said. "When Matthew makes his mind up about somethin', there's no getting him to change it. By times he's stubborn as a government mule an' then some."

Matt struggled into his sheepskin and settled his hat on his head. "Now don't you go worrying about me, Kitty." He smiled. "Remember that small worries cast some mighty giant shadows."

"Small worries! You've got a broken leg and you're going up against four gunmen." Kitty stepped closer to him. "I wouldn't say that's a small worry."

Deciding that his talking was done, Matt turned to Festus. "Take care of her," he said. Then quickly he opened the door and stomped into the deepening day, leaving Kitty openmouthed and fuming.

Lou Carlson helped Matt saddle his bay and for once the liveryman asked no questions, the grim set of the marshal's jaw warning him that now wasn't the time. For his part, Buck didn't object to Matt mounting from the right and the big horse seemed rested and eager for the trail.

"Keep my crutch until I get back, Lou," Matt said. He touched his hat brim. "Until later, amigo."

Matt rode clear of Front Street, not wanting to be seen by Henry, coming up on the bridge over the frozen Arkansas from behind the Dodge House.

He cleared the river and swung due west along the southern bank, riding into a white wilderness of snow, the drifts piled up here and there like icebergs in a polar sea.

The wheels of the heavy wagons had cut deep into the snow, leaving a trail that was easy to follow. After three miles the wheel ruts swung away from the river and headed southwest and Matt followed. He crossed several narrow, icebound streams and found himself in flat, rolling country.

Around him lay desolation, an unbroken carpet of dazzling white stretching to the horizon. Here and there spiky yucca raised snow-spattered leaves to the sky, and around some of the draws off the creek, cottonwoods spread their smooth, bare limbs and shivered in the cold.

The day was well advanced, but the sky was still blue with only a few white clouds

to the north and the yellow sun
bright but offered no warmth. Mat
hunched into his coat, his breath sm
wishful for a riding boot on his left f
stead of just a damp sock with a hole
toe. There was no question of usi
stirrup, and his broken leg hung
hurting now from the motion of the h

The big bay, Montana bred for
country, pushed ahead at a good
white plumes lifting from his cru
hooves as he high-stepped acros
frozen prairie.

Matt scanned the country ahead. H
a man well used to searching across
distances, but the dazzling white
snow under the bright glare of th
hazed all the way to the horizon, bu
his eyes so he had to squint to mak
the trail ahead.

He saw nothing but the tracks
wagons, vanishing into a vast, empty
that looked lonely and lost amid the
less winter.

After another mile, Matt rode up
spot where the four Henry gunmen
split away from the wagon trail and le
to the north, back in the direction
Arkansas.

Their motive was easy to figure.

sh   ned to swing ahead of the
t roa   reach the train before the
oking,   nce there, intimidating the
ot in-   ngers with their guns, they
in the   l and then hightail it back
g the
loose,   as determined not to let
orse.

snow   he trail left by the horse-
pace,   bling into a drift that rose
ching   e the flat, deep enough to
s the   bay trouble.

ndered through the drift,
e was   the outlaw's trail again.
great   s had turned southwest,
f the   for the Santa Fe tracks.
sun   caught sight of the file of
rning   matching alongside the
e out   nem tilted drunkenly from
e blizzard, downed wires
f the   snow.

land   of the four Henry men
end-   not far ahead of him. From
of the outlaw's gang, all
n the   es who looked like they'd
had   are of killing. Such men
oped   ely to give up without going
f the

gainst one, but he'd bucked
The   odds before. Still, the long

hours before a gun battle pace themselves slowly and give a man time to think. If he's a doubting kind of man, there is always the chance he'll turn away from the fight, the courage draining out of him like sand though an hourglass.

But Matt Dillon was not a doubting man. No matter the odds, he had come this far to do what had to be done. There would be no turning back.

Now he was close enough to spot the outlaws in the distance, riding two abreast near the rails, which were clear of snow in only a few places.

The riders were walking their horses, talking to one another, realizing well the slowness of Kelley's wagons. They had plenty of time to reach the train and abduct Isobel Charles-Greenwood before the rescuers got there.

Matt turned in the saddle and glanced behind him. There was no sign of the mayor's rescue party. The big freight wagons must have been making slow progress through the deeper drifts and their wheels probably had to be dug out in places.

The marshal knew he could expect no help from Kelley.

Only a quarter mile separated Matt from

Henry's men when they spotted him on their back trail. The riders conferred briefly, then reined up and turned to face him. Out here in the open, there was no cover of any kind. This would be a rifle and revolver duel from horseback, long-distance work, and it would be very easy to wash out, very easy to die.

His eyes fixed on Henry's men, Matt pulled off his thick leather gloves and blew on his hands and began to work the stiffness from them. He leaned over and slid the Winchester from the boot under his knee and levered a round into the chamber. That done he laid the rifle across the saddle horn and slipped the rawhide thong from his Colt.

The four riders ahead of him stood their horses, waiting, their confidence apparent in the relaxed, easy way they sat their saddles. This was nothing new to these men. It was something they'd faced before, perhaps many times.

Matt realized this would be a repeat of the fight he and Festus had with the McCarty brothers — only this time he was trying to buck the odds with an even colder deck.

But there was no other way. The four outlaws ahead of him were fighting men, not talkers, all gurgle and no guts. They would go to the gun and they'd be good — and almighty sudden.

Matt, the sound of his thumping heart loud in his ears, urged the bay forward, rode to within a hundred yards of the bandits and reined up. "You men!" he yelled. "Surrender now and I'll see you all get a fair trial on the charges of bank robbery and murder."

One of the men laughed, turned to his companions and said something and they laughed with him. The four were dressed in thick woolen mackinaws and a couple had mufflers pulled over their hats, tied under their chins. All had rifles at the ready; they looked to Matt like a mean and determined bunch without any backup in them.

One of the outlaws, the bearded man named Tom, who had kicked Matt's crutch out from under him at the Long Branch, stood in the stirrups, put an open palm to the side of his mouth and hollered, "You toddle on home now, lawman, an' let us be about our business."

"While you still can," a young towhead yelled, grinning, his mouth steaming in the cruel cold.

The outlaws expected Matt to talk, perhaps try to reason with them. But the marshal had said his piece and he knew there was no more talking to be done. Instead, he did the very opposite of what they expected. He dug a spur into the bay, yelled a loud, meaningless war cry and charged.

Matt threw his rifle to his shoulder and the gun roared and spat fire. The bearded man went down with his horse, both floundering into the snow in a tangle of legs and stirrups. Matt fired again at the others. A miss. But the spiteful whine of the bullet served to split up the three remaining horsemen. One headed over the tracks while the other two broke to the marshal's right.

The outlaws were caught flat-footed, the speed and ferocity of Matt's attack taking them completely by surprise. One man doesn't ride against four. It shouldn't have been happening this way.

A bullet tugged at Matt's sleeve as he rode closer. The deep snow slowed the speed of his charge, but even so, the bay was covering the ground at a good pace.

At a distance of twenty yards, the marshal yanked the rifle from his shoulder and hammered shot after shot at the outlaws, firing rapidly from the hip, a rippling arc of ejected brass shells tumbling into the snow.

A man, hit hard, bent over and clutched the saddle horn, blood staining the front of his mackinaw. He stayed in place for a few moments; then his eyes rolled in his head and he tumbled out of the saddle.

The towhead, his face gray and frightened, tossed away his Winchester, threw up his hands and yelled something the marshal didn't hear. All Matt's attention was now on the outlaw who had crossed the rails. The man fired and the bullet buzzed angrily past Matt's cheek. The marshal swung around in the saddle and fired, fired again. Hit twice the outlaw screamed, slid from his horse, thudded into the snow and lay still.

"I'm out of it!" the towhead called out, eyes bright with fear in his white face. "For God's sake, don't shoot no more. I'm done."

Through a sullen gray drift of powder smoke, Matt looked at the carnage around him. In less than ten ticks of the watch in his vest pocket, three men and a horse were down. Two of the outlaws lay dead in the snow and the third, the bearded man, was on his hands and knees, gut shot, coughing up black blood.

"You!" Matt called to the towhead. "Unbuckle your gun belt and let it fall to the ground." The kid did as he was told, and the marshal asked: "What's your name, boy?"

"Danny Gannon," the youngster answered. He nodded to the bearded man. "That's my brother, Tom, and I wish to God we'd never left Texas."

"See to him," Matt said.

Gannon swung out of the saddle, but even as he did, his brother rattled deep in his throat and fell to his right, his eyes wide but seeing nothing.

The towhead stopped and looked up at Matt sitting tall and terrible in the saddle. "I never saw a man shoot a rifle that fast," he said. "None of us, except Deke Waters maybe, pegged you for any kind of a gunfighter."

"You should have listened to Waters," Matt said. "That's the trouble about picking on a man you don't know, boy — you never can tell what you're going to get."

Gannon looked around him. "Well, we got ten different kinds of hell. You played hob, lawman."

"You spoke to Waters," Matt said, not an ounce of give in him. "You were advised."

Chapter 11

The Billionaire's Daughter

"May all the saints in Heaven preserve us and save us, what in God's holy name happened here?"

Mayor Kelley, his face sick with shock, looked around at the dead men, their blood staining scarlet on the snow, and with a trembling hand reached into his coat for a cigar.

"These are Scar Henry's boys," Matt said. "Three dead" — he nodded toward Gannon — "and him." The marshal waited until Kelley had lit his cigar, then added: "They came after Isobel What's-her-name."

"Charles-Greenwood," the mayor said absently, his horrified eyes on Tom Gannon curled on the ground.

Several other townsmen had gathered around Kelley and they constantly looked back and forth from the dead outlaws to the marshal, their gaze breaking away quickly when they met Matt's level eyes. These were civilized men trying very hard to grasp the enormity of the destruction they were seeing, and they could only guess at the manner of the man who had wrought such havoc.

All were familiar with weapons and most had used them in the past, but the gun skill possessed by the big, hard-boned marshal was outside their experience and beyond their understanding.

It was a gift given to perhaps one man in ten thousand, and maybe in a hundred thousand, to have the coordination between hand and eye to use a gun as expertly as Matt Dillon did that day. That was the reason why, of all the millions of men who carried arms in the West from the end of the War Between the States to the closing of the frontier, the number of truly great gunfighters numbered less than a hundred.

Such men were rare, and even more rarely encountered by the average citizen. But when chanced upon, either by happenstance or sheer ill luck, they were best left alone.

Now the men around Kelley could only look and wonder, conflicting emotions tangled up in their faces, none of them desirous to again meet the cold gunmetal gray eyes of the lawman on the big bay horse.

Kelley was first to recover his composure and he turned to the surviving outlaw. "What's your name, boy?"

Gannon told him, and the mayor said: "I'll see you get a fair trial and a first-class hanging. No expense will be spared, mind you. A new hemp rope, no hand-me-downs, and a good, honest six-foot drop, measured right."

"That's my brother over there," Gannon said as though he hadn't heard, his eyes slanting to the dead man in the snow. "We should've stayed in Texas."

Kelley beamed. "Words as true as were ever spoken, me boy. But now it's time to play the man and take your medicine."

The mayor looked up at Matt in the saddle, watching him thumb shells from his cartridge belt and feed them into the Winchester. "How far to the train, do you reckon, Marshal?"

"Not far," Matt answered. "Maybe a couple of miles down the track."

"Then let's get going. Those wagons are almighty slow."

Matt reached behind him into his saddlebags and came up with a set of shackles. "Slap these onto Gannon's wrists, Mayor. Then get him up on his horse."

Kelley did as he was told, locking the

irons behind the young outlaw's back.

"You're a careful man, aren't you, Marshal Dillon?" Kelley said. "And I'd say an unforgiving one."

Matt nodded, his face set and grim. "Live longer that way."

Taking one last look around him at the dead, Kelley swung into the saddle and waved the wagons forward. Matt followed behind the rear wagon, Gannon riding, head bent, a couple of yards in front of him.

They reached the stranded train an hour later.

Winter travelers to Dodge City and points east were few and the train consisted of only a locomotive, two passenger cars, a single boxcar and a caboose.

The track curved at that point and the ties had been laid across an ancient dry wash, which had caught and held the snow and caused it to drift much higher here than on the surrounding flat.

It seemed to Matt that the locomotive had slowed as it labored to buck through the drift. As the engineer applied more steam to build up speed, the engine had shoved more and more snow in front of it. Finally the snow had piled so high in an icy wall, even the powerful locomotive could no longer push it aside and roll forward. The big iron wheels had spun uselessly on the icy track and had finally ground to a halt.

A parapet of snow was heaped ahead of the locomotive almost to the height of the lantern at the base of the huge, bell-shaped smoke stack and a thick layer of ice had formed between the wheels and the rails.

The entire train was frozen to the tracks and it would take several engines to break it free.

Someone, probably the fireman, had cleared a space around the lead passenger car and a drift of smoke rose from its stove chimney. When the wagons rolled into sight, pale, anxious faces appeared at the frost-laced windows, and from inside, Matt heard a few voices raised in a feeble cheer.

The engineer and fireman dropped from the back of the car and stumbled through deep snow to greet Kelley. The engineer, a big-bellied man with the florid face of a drinker grinned and waved to the mayor. "Name's McIntyre, and are we glad to see you," he said. "Firewood's almost gone and the passengers are starting to get mighty cold. I reckoned by tomorrow morning we'd begin to count our dead."

"How many on board?" Kelley asked.

"Fifteen," McIntyre answered, "three of them women, one pushing eighty if she's a day."

Kelley leaned forward in the saddle. "Do you have a Mrs. Isobel Charles-Greenwood on board?"

The engineer nodded. "I should say. At every stop down the line, somebody made a point of telling us that her father is a major shareholder of this railroad."

"Please ask the lady if she would honor Mayor James Kelley of Dodge City with her presence," Kelley said. "At her convenience of course."

After McIntyre left and the mayor's volunteers began carrying blankets and food into the car, Kelley turned, looked down at Matt's foot and made a face. "Is that the best sock you have?" he asked. "It's hardly fitting attire to meet Mrs. Charles-Greenwood."

Matt wiggled his toes and glanced at the hole. "Right now, Mayor, it's the only sock I have."

Kelley shook his head, exasperated. "Then, for Heaven's sake, keep it out of sight, man. Cover it up or something." He looked over to Gannon, who was sitting sullen and silent in the saddle. "And do something with him. The very sight of a desperate outlaw might make the young lady faint dead away."

"Want me to shoot him, Mayor?" Matt asked.

"That's not funny, Marshal," Kelly snorted. He opened his mouth to say more but closed it quickly when he saw the attentive engineer assist a beautiful, vacant china doll from the car, all baby blue eyes, corn silk hair and porcelain skin.

"Remember the sock," he hissed from the corner of his mouth before he swung out of the saddle, rushed to meet the woman and bent over her hand. "This is indeed an honor, Mrs. Charles-Greenwood. My name is James Kelley, Mayor of Dodge City, and may I say, with all due modesty I hope, the leader of your intrepid rescuers."

The girl dropped a slight, but well-bred, curtsy and wrapped her blanket closer around her shapely body. "You arrived at a most opportune time, Mr. Mayor. I confess, the thought of spending another freezing night in that carriage had me quite undone." Isobel batted long lashes over her empty eyes and added: "As you can understand I am most anxious to continue my journey to Fort Dodge, where my husband awaits me."

"And with a great deal of impatience, I'll be bound." Kelley beamed. "Young love knows how precious are the golden moments since they fly by so fast."

"Quite," Isobel said, her voice flat.

As a silence stretched long and finally into mild embarrassment, the mayor beckoned to Matt, who kneed his horse forward, bringing Gannon with him. "Mrs. Charles-Greenwood, may I introduce Marshal Matt Dillon of Dodge."

Matt touched his hat brim and the girl nodded without interest. "Oh dear," she said absently, "he has a hole in his sock."

"Ah yes, ahem, but he plans to find another one directly," Kelley assured her, angling a hard look at the marshal.

"And who is that man?" she asked.

"Who, him? Oh, he's a dangerous outlaw that Marshal Dillon captured after a desperate encounter just a short while ago."

"He does look dangerous," Isobel said. She touched her tongue to her top lip. "And very wild."

For the first time since their meeting, Matt saw something akin to animation in the girl's insipid eyes. Isobel lifted the hem of her gray wool traveling dress and stepped lightly beside Gannon's horse.

"Be careful, ma'am," Matt warned.

"Like the mayor said, this man is dangerous and he can be almighty sudden."

Gannon, hard-eyed and handsome, a shock of blond hair falling over his forehead from under his hat, looked down at the woman with surly fascination.

Isobel reached out and lightly placed the tips of her fingers on Gannon's thigh. Then she quickly pulled her hand away again as though she'd touched something hot.

"He is wild." The girl shivered, her breath coming in short, agitated gasps. "And he . . . he smells and looks like an animal. I've never seen an outlaw before."

"And he's violent and treacherous like all his kind," Kelley said, his puzzled eyes lifting to Matt's. "Please step away from him, Mrs. Charles-Greenwood. You are in some danger there."

The girl did as she was told. She walked to Kelley and, as though nothing untoward had happened, said: "As I told you, Mr. Mayor, I am most anxious to continue on to Fort Dodge right away. I'm sure my husband is becoming most apprehensive."

"But I wouldn't hear of it, ma'am." Kelley beamed. "After your ordeal on the train, I insist that you spend the night at my home. Mrs. Kelley will make you very welcome."

"But I —"

"Please," the mayor interrupted, "let me beg you to accept my hospitality. You'll be better rested to make the journey to the fort tomorrow morning." He shrugged apologetically. "It's only a few miles, but I fear the snow will make it a most arduous trip." Kelley glanced at the sky. "Besides, dear lady, it will be well dark by the time we reach Dodge, not a good hour for a well-bred lady to undertake onerous travel."

Isobel's pretty face frowned in thought, then cleared. She smiled and dropped another curtsy. "I bow to your more mature judgment, Mr. Mayor, though I hope Mrs. Kelley will not think my maid and myself an intolerable burden."

"Not at all." Kelley beamed again. "Like me, she will be honored. In fact, I believe you may be able to talk her into baking one of her famous apple-and-raisin pies. She has won a blue ribbon many times for that pie." The mayor hesitated, a sly, calculating expression creeping over his face. "And, of course, I can supply pen and paper so that you may write your father and tell him of your adventure and your safe return to Dodge." He coughed slightly and refused to look at Matt, who was staring hard at him, a smile tugging at his mouth. "Only if you wish, of course, but you may care to mention that I led the rescue party. Kelley, by the way, is spelled K-E-L-L-E-Y. First name, James."

"I will make certain my father knows of your rescue, Mayor Kelley. I am sure he will be most grateful." The girl drew up the blanket that had slipped from her shoulders and said: "Now, if you will excuse me, I have to get some things from the train. And my maid of course. She's a tiresome girl, but good servants are hard to find these days."

"Yes, indeed, madam," Kelley said, shaking his head sadly, like one who had firsthand knowledge of the vagaries of servants. He waved toward the wagons, where blanket-wrapped passengers were already being loaded. "I am sorry I can offer you no better conveyance than a humble freight wagon."

Isobel glanced at the wagons and sniffed. "Then a wagon will just have to do, won't it?" From under her lashes, the girl slanted one last, lingering look at Gannon, then turned on her heel and, skirt lifted high above shapely ankles, stepped back to the train.

"Fine girl, fine girl in every way." Kelley smiled at Matt. "I think breeding always tells, don't you?"

The marshal let the question go without reply, but said: "Mayor, do you think it wise to take Mrs. What's-her-name to your house? She'd be a lot safer in the marshal's office."

Kelley waved a dismissive hand. "I always have my Colt's Dragoon close to hand. Besides, I don't think even Scar Henry would dare attack the home of the honorable mayor of Dodge City."

"Don't count on it," Matt said. "He's done a sight worse."

Chapter 12

Temptation of the Gunman

Scar Henry and Deacon Waters were standing on the boardwalk outside the Long Branch when Kelley led his wagons past the saloon to the Dodge House.

Matt and Gannon sat their horses outside the marshal's office, and after a few moments, Festus opened the door, the Greener in his left hand.

Matt nodded to the outlaw. "One of Henry's boys. Take him inside and lock him up, Festus. I'm heading for the livery stable."

"Four rode out, Matthew," the deputy said. "Where are the others?"

"They won't be coming back," Matt replied.

Festus read the rest of the answer to his question in the big marshal's eyes and saw no need to press the matter. "You, get down from there." He motioned to Gannon with the Greener. "And take it real easy. This here scattergun has a hair trigger an' by times I'm a mighty nervous man."

The outlaw threw a bitter curse at Matt and climbed out of the saddle. Then Festus none too gently prodded him inside, passing Kitty in the doorway.

"Matt, are you all right?" she asked. "I've been worried sick."

"I'm fine," the marshal answered, a bone-weary tiredness in him. "Now get back inside. I'll return real soon."

"But, Matt —"

"Get inside, Kitty."

Matt's tone left no room for argument and Kitty nodded. "Just be careful."

The marshal touched his hat brim and swung his horse away from the office, but he reined up when Henry called out from across the street.

"Hey, you, Dillon! Where are the rest of my men?"

"Dead," Matt answered. He jerked a thumb over his shoulder. "Except for him. I'm saving him for a hanging."

Henry's jaw dropped. "Who killed my boys?"

"I did," Matt said. "They were duly notified, but still refused to give me the road."

"Damn you, Dillon!" Henry yelled, his face black with rage. "I'll make you pay for this. I'll make this whole sorry town pay."

Matt's own anger flared. He pushed his

coat away from his gun. "Then let's end it, Henry!" he hollered. "You sorry piece of trash, shuck your iron and we'll end it right here and now."

Waters, a careful man, split a little to Henry's left, his eyes, quiet and confident, fixed on the big lawman.

Henry thought about it. He thought long and hard.

The huge reflectors behind the oil lamps along Front Street splashed bronze light across the churned-up snow like wet paint, and the gusting wind carried an icy warning of more bad weather to come. The wind lifted a flapping sheet of newspaper high into the air between Matt and Henry before letting it flutter to the ground like a stricken dove. Matt heard voices from the direction of the Dodge House and from further away a dog barked once and fell silent. High above the town the sky was darkening with cloud, and one by one the stars were going out.

Matt was tense, ready, his exhaustion and the throbbing pain in his leg a spur to his anger. He had made up his mind. He would shoot at Waters first, then, if he was able to take the hits and keep firing, at Henry.

He had no illusions. The moment was

coming when he'd earn his wages the hard way, fulfilling his obligation to this town with his life.

On the boardwalk, Henry was wound tight, a man obviously considering his options. Maybe it was the way Matt sat his horse, his hand close to his long-barreled Colt, that gave him pause. That and the fact that the big lawman had killed three of his men, all of them gun handy. A realist, the outlaw would know that at a range of just ten yards he would attract some accurate lead.

He could die — and now that he was doing so well, death was not part of his plans.

"Here, what's going on?"

Mayor Kelley plodded toward them through the snow leading his horse. Isobel Charles-Greenwood was up in the saddle, wrapped in a green velvet cloak, and her thin, young maid trailed behind on foot, lugging a couple of carpetbags, which seemed way too heavy for her.

Kelley stopped midway between Matt and Henry, and both men knew the moment had passed. So did Waters. The gunman strolled back to the door of the saloon and stood facing Matt, his hands well away from his guns. Now that the issue of the gunfight was over, he seemed to have little interest in what came next.

"You hold right there, Mayor," Henry said. "I want to talk to you."

The outlaw turned his head, said something to Waters, and the man ducked inside the Long Branch. He appeared a few moments later with Doc, Sam Noonan and the five hostage townsmen, the other surviving outlaw covering them with his rifle.

One man had a rope around his neck. That man was Doc Adams, his bruised face showing the result of a recent beating.

"Listen good, Mayor, and you too, Dillon," Henry said. "I'm upping the ante. You both be here at first light tomorrow and I'll give you my demands. If they ain't met, we'll hang the pill roller at noon, and one man every hour thereafter." Henry pointed to a pulley beam that jutted from the front of the saloon; it was used to lift heavy beer barrels off the delivery wagons. "We'll hang 'em from there, in full view of the whole damn town."

Kelley seemed lost for words. Matt saw the man trying to come to terms with what was happening, looking for a way out. The bleak expression that passed across the mayor's face revealed that he did not find one.

Henry, seeing Kelley as a beaten man, dismissed him, his gaze flickering to Isobel. "What you say, little lady?" He leered. "Want to leave these rubes and come inside an' join us? You and me, we can go upstairs and have ourselves a little fun."

The girl flushed and Kelley took the cigar from his mouth and threw it angrily into the snow. "Now listen here," he said, "this is Mrs. Charles-Greenwood. Her husband is an officer at Fort Dodge, and her father is a mighty rich and important man."

"I know who she is," Henry said, his hungry eyes on the girl. His black stare went to Matt. "I had three men killed today because I know who she is."

Kelley opened his mouth to speak but couldn't find his voice. He shook his head, gathered the reins of his horse and led it forward.

As Isobel passed Henry, her eyes were no longer downcast — they were on the outlaw. Matt saw them travel slowly from the top of his hat to the toes of his boots, lingering for a few moments on the terrible scar across his cheek. Henry saw that look, knew what it implied and grinned. He said something to Waters and both men laughed. Isobel flushed again and quickly dropped her eyes.

Isobel Charles-Greenwood, Matt decided, was one mighty strange woman.

And maybe one that would bear watching.

Matt rode into the livery stable and was pleased to see that Lou Carlson had left his crutch where it would be handy, next to Buck's stall.

The big marshal swung out of the saddle and stood on one leg while he unsaddled the bay. He used the crutch to hobble to the oat sack, where he scooped a bait for the horse, then forked him some hay.

"Not an easy job for a one-legged man."

Deacon Waters' voice came from behind him and Matt froze.

"Relax, Marshal," the gunman said, a smile in the words. "I'm not here to hunt trouble. Besides, I got no need to gun you in the back. I can do that pretty well from the front."

Matt turned slowly, clearing his coat from his Colt. Waters stood loose and easy, mackinaw drawn back, his thumbs tucked into his gun belt. His startling ice blue eyes were quiet but alert, missing nothing.

"Why are you here, Waters?" Matt asked. "I doubt it's a social call."

The gunman shrugged. "Can't really say why I'm here because I don't rightly know my ownself. Call it a whim if you like."

"Did you plan on shooting me in the back?"

Waters smiled and shook his head. "Like I already told you, I can take you from the front any day of the week. Backshooting isn't my style."

"I wonder if the girl you killed thought that," Matt said, his voice hard and uncompromising. "Seems to me, she had your bullet in her back."

If Waters was stung, he didn't let it show. "She was nothing. A two-dollar whore who shacked up with her pimp. Women in general are no account, and women like that even less."

"Why are you here, Waters?" Matt asked again, realizing that he was talking to a man without a soul, lacking even a trace of humanity.

The gunman's cold smile withered as he chose to ignore the marshal's question. "Back there outside the saloon, you wanted to kill me real bad, didn't you?"

Matt nodded. "I figured you first, then Henry."

"Bad idea," Waters said. "I'd have shot

you out of the saddle before you even cleared leather."

"Maybe," Matt said. "Maybe not."

"Depend on it," Waters said. "Nobody is faster with a gun than me. There was no one before and there will be no one afterward. I'm what your smart doctor friend might call a phenomenon."

"Or a freak," Matt said, pushing it. "Do I have to stand here listening to you bragging on yourself all night, or will you give me the road?" he asked, taking a hobbling step toward the gunman.

Again Waters seemed to take no offense and let the question go. "Get back on your horse, Dillon," he said. "Move to a different range until this thing is over."

"Thanks for the advice, but I reckon I'll stick," Matt said.

Waters shook his head. "How much do they pay you, huh? Eighty a month maybe? Is eighty a month worth dying for?"

A wry smile touched Matt's mouth. "Waters, you seem mighty interested in my well-being. Since that's the case, I have a proposition for you. Why don't you and Henry step over to the marshal's office and turn in your guns? I'll make sure you both get a fair trial and a fine hanging."

"Not going to happen," Waters said. "See,

Dave Henry has big plans. One of them is that he aims to kill you before he leaves."

"He'll get his chance," Matt said. "Fact is, I'm looking forward to it."

Waters nodded. "It will be a close thing, I reckon. Ol' Dave is pretty quick with the Colt." The gunman still blocked Matt's path to the door and made no move to get out of the way. "You made me a proposition, and now I'll make you one," Waters said. "Tie in with me. We'd be a team, you and me. This is your chance to make some real money, more money in a month than you'd make in a lifetime as an eighty-a-month star strutter."

"How about your boss?" Matt asked. "Seems to me only a buzzard feeds on his friends."

"Who, Dave? He's a business associate, not a friend. Once I get my share of the cash from the banks, him and me will part company. Hell, Dillon, I'll gun him if you want. Then we'd have the whole shebang to ourselves. We can head down Mexico way, or any other place that takes your fancy. Maybe some jerkwater town with a big, fat bank just begging to be robbed." Excitement flamed in Waters' eyes. "Think about it, Dillon. Me and you, just consider the possibilities."

"Why are you offering me this, Waters?" Matt asked, leading the man.

"Because I like your style. You're smart, you got guts and you rode with wild ones before. But more to the point, you have class — something ol' Dave will never have."

Matt nodded and bowed his head, as though thinking things through. Then he raised his eyes to Waters, eyes as cold and unforgiving as frozen bullets. "Waters," he said, "I'll see you in Hell first. Sure I make tin-star wages, but I come by them honestly. I'd willingly starve before I'd ride the owlhoot trail with a woman-killing, back-shooting piece of scum like you. Those wild ones you talk about, they were men, not two-bit, sure-thing killers hunting notches. Hell, since you walked into this barn, I can't even bear to breathe the same air you breathe. The very sight of you makes me sick to my stomach." Matt's hand dropped close to his gun. "Now clear the hell out of my way and give me the road."

Apart for the tightening of the skin across his cheekbones, Waters' expression didn't change. The most tangible sign that Matt's words had hit home was the hardness that had shaded into the gunman's eyes.

"I showed you the way, Dillon, gave you your chance," he said. "You won't ever get another."

Waters turned away and stepped toward the barn door. Then suddenly he spun around, his guns flashing clear of the holsters. Two shots at the same instant. Two .44 bullets smashed into the bottom of Matt's crutch, the hard pine exploding into a hundred flying splinters. The marshal had not cleared leather, and now he had no chance to complete the draw. The crutch gave way and he crashed heavily on his back, a jolt of pain shooting through his leg like a lightning bolt.

For a few moments Matt lay on the floor stunned. He heard Waters step toward him, the gunman's spurs chiming like bells. Waters holstered the revolver in his left hand, then reached down and took Matt's gun and threw it across the barn.

"Next time I draw down on you, Dillon, and there will be a next time very soon, I'll kill you," he said.

The big Russian revolver in Waters' hand spun, a gleaming disk of blue steel, then thudded into the holster. The gunman's eyes lowered and fixed on Matt once last time. Then, his face bunched up with a mix of hate and contempt, he turned on his heel and walked out of the barn.

The big marshal raised himself to a sitting position, his broken leg straight out in front of him. He lifted the remains of his crutch and sadly shook his head. "I wonder," he said to himself aloud, "where Lou put that spare crutch."

Matt struggled to his feet and, using the wall of the barn as support, hopped his way to Lou Carlson's tiny office. As he'd hoped, the crutch was propped in a corner. Matt retrieved the crutch and tucked it into his left armpit.

The big marshal thudded his way across the barn, picked up his gun and made his way to the livery stable door.

It was snowing again.

Chapter 13

Money and Women

The gunsmith Newly O'Brien was a bachelor who lived in a small room at the rear of his store. Matt left the barn and made his way there.

This was no blizzard, but the snow fell steadily, driven by a keening wind, and the night was bitter cold. There were few people on the street, and those there hurried about their business, seeing nothing, wrapped to the eyes in furs or woolens.

A coyote, driven by hunger to forage in town, slunk from an alley and stood in the marshal's path, its grin sly. Matt didn't slow his pace. "You git," he said.

The coyote dropped its tail between its legs and faded back into the darkness, giving the big human the road.

Matt pounded on the door of O'Brien's store, waited a couple of minutes, then tried again. From deep within a man yelled: "Go away. I'm closed. This ain't hunting or fishing weather anyhow. Come back tomorrow, or in the spring."

"Newly," the marshal hollered, "it's Matt Dillon. I have to talk with you. It's important."

A bolt slammed back and the door opened a few inches. One eye appeared and, below that, the glint of something blue. "Oh, it is you, Matt," O'Brien said. He opened the door wider. "Come inside. I have coffee that's just on the bile."

Thirty minutes later, Matt left the gunsmith's parlor and headed through a shifting curtain of white back to his office.

"Matt, what took you so long?" Kitty asked, stepping quickly to his side. "I was starting to get really concerned." She looked him over and exclaimed: "I declare, you're frozen stiff!"

The marshal shrugged out of his coat, hung that and his hat on the rack, then stumped to the desk. "Had a run-in with Deke Waters," he said, accepting a cup of coffee from Kitty.

"What happened, Matthew?" Festus asked.

"Shot my crutch out from under me," Matt answered. He laid a hand on the one propped against his desk. "This is my spare."

"But . . . but" — Kitty's eyes showed her confusion — "why did he do that?"

"He figured he had his reasons, I guess. I have to hand it to him. Waters is fast — the fastest man with a gun I've ever seen." Matt touched the crutch again. "And he hits what he aims at."

"Skunk bushwhacked you, huh?" Festus asked.

Matt shook his head. "I had my chance. I just wasn't fast enough."

"That's because of your broke leg an' all, Matthew. It's slowed you some." Hope gleamed in the deputy's eyes. "Ain't that right? I mean, that the leg has slowed you some."

"Maybe," Matt answered. Then, allowing Festus a measure of comfort: "Could be the broke leg has slowed me." He nodded. "Uh-huh, sure could be."

"A misery can wear on a man," the deputy said, "make him a heap slower than he really is. Seen it time after time."

Matt let it go, sealing his lips with his coffee cup.

"Somebody comin'," Festus said from his place at the window. "It's Jed Owens."

Festus stepped to the door and let the man inside. The banker brushed snow off his shoulders, touched his hat to Kitty and got right to the point. "Marshal, I'm very concerned about Jane Morgan. My missus says she refuses to eat or drink and just sits in a chair, staring at the wall. She doesn't talk or shed a tear, and as far as I know, she hasn't slept since her husband was killed."

"Mr. Owens, what can we do?" Kitty asked, her eyes troubled.

"I don't think there's anything we can do," Owens answered. "She needs a doctor. I went to Doc Adams' place, but he's not there."

"You mean you haven't heard?" Festus asked.

"Heard what?"

"Maybe you'd better tell him, Matthew," Festus said.

Matt told Owens about Doc going into the Long Branch to treat the wounded men and being kept hostage himself. Deciding to keep nothing back, Matt added: "Scar Henry says he'll hang Doc tomorrow at noon unless his demands are met."

"Then we must meet them, Marshal," Owens declared. "The bank's money doesn't matter, not when a good man's life is at stake."

"Glad to hear you say that, Jed," Matt said. "But I won't let them hang Doc, and I will get your money back."

"You have a plan?" Owens asked hopefully.

"Maybe," Matt answered. "Mayor Kelley and me will talk to Henry at first light tomorrow. I'll know better after then."

Owens sighed. "I do hope this business is resolved soon. Poor Mrs. Morgan is so far gone in grief, I fear for her life."

Kitty opened her mouth to speak, but Matt headed her off. "No, Kitty. You can't go crossing the tracks. Doc will see Jane Morgan soon. I promise you."

"I hope you're right, Marshal." Owens sighed. "Time is running out."

"For all of us," Matt said.

After Owens left, Festus stood at his post by the window deep in thought. Finally he turned to Matt and said: "You know, Mathew, I've been thinkin' an' I have a plan. See, ol' Scar is down to just hisself an' two other men. What say when them rannies come out to hang Doc, we just lay for 'em here an' pick 'em off?"

"It's a plan, Festus," Matt said, "and I did study on it some myself. The trouble is, Henry will make sure he's shielded by Sam Noonan and the other prisoners. If we start shooting we could hit a lot of innocent men." Matt shrugged. "We'd have to drop all three of those outlaws at one time. Otherwise they'd start killing." Matt's eyes searched his deputy's strained, pale face. "Figure you can shoot well enough with one hand off your left shoulder to hit what you aim at?"

"I don't reckon, Matthew," Festus said, looking crestfallen. "Maybe my plan isn't as good as I figured."

"Keep on thinking, Festus." Matt smiled. "Could be you'll come up with something better." He hesitated, then added: "Or maybe I will."

Matt and Kitty slept for a few hours while Festus stood guard. Then, a couple of hours before daybreak, the marshal took his place at the window.

Outside the snow was still falling, the tumbling flakes reflecting in the light of the oil lamps. Over at the Long Branch all was quiet, but an hour into his watch, Matt saw Waters step outside and look around. The gunman glanced over at the office, then walked back inside the saloon.

Like himself, Waters was waiting for the dawn.

The sky was still dark when Mayor Kelley thumped along the boardwalk and pounded on the door. Matt let the man inside and Kelley brushed snow from his coat and without a word stepped to the coffeepot on the stove. He poured himself a cup, tasted, grimaced, then growled: "Has that damned scoundrel shown his face yet?"

Matt shook his head. "Still half an hour until first light, Mayor. You're early."

Kelley, looking grumpy and ill at ease, seemed like he was ready to say something, but changed his mind, lapsing into silence.

Guessing at the cause of the mayor's ill humor, Matt gave him an opening. "How's Mrs. Charles-Greenwood?"

Kelley eagerly seized on the opportunity. "Matt, she's a demanding, unreasonable woman. She ran that poor maid of hers ragged last night, wanting this and that: a shawl, a book, a cup of tea. The maid's name is Nancy and she's a plain little thing. But you should see the look on her face sometimes when she looks at Mrs. Charles-Greenwood. Such a look of pure hatred, it made my blood run cold."

Kelley turned wounded, unbelieving eyes to the marshal. "Listen to this. Mrs. Isobel Charles-Greenwood took one bite of Mrs. Kelley's apple-and-raisin pie and shoved the plate away from her. Said she didn't care for it." The mayor slowly shook his head, baffled by the enormity of the outrage. "Can you imagine? Mrs. Kelley, poor woman, goes out of her way to bake her famous blue-ribbon pie, and Mrs. Isobel Charles-Greenwood doesn't care for it."

"Your wife bakes a powerful good pie, Mayor," Matt said, trying to soothe the man. "I could use a wedge of it right now. Seems all I've eaten for days is beans and canned peaches."

Kelley nodded absently. "Right, right, Marshal. I'll see you get what's left." He looked through the gun slit at the falling snow. "The thing of it is, I may have that woman for a week if this damned foul weather keeps up."

"Maybe you'll get lucky and her husband will come fetch her," Matt said.

"I hope so, Matt." Kelley sighed, spreading helpless hands. "How I do hope so."

The long night slowly shaded to an uncertain dawn, the sullen gray light brightened only by the falling snow. Over at the Long Branch men stirred and Henry, Waters and the other outlaw led a shuffling file of captives onto the boardwalk outside.

Doc Adams still had the rope around his neck, and Waters, careful to shield himself from the marshal's office with dejected townsmen, led him to a spot under the pulley beam. He let down the pulley, threaded the rope through the groove of the sheave, then hoisted it up again. Waters, grinning, held on to the end of the rope and yanked hard so the noose around Doc's neck tightened and the physician grimaced in pain.

Henry watched until this was done, then stepped to the edge of the walk and cupped his hands around his mouth. "Matt Dillon!" he yelled. "It's time to have our talk!"

"Ready, Mayor?" Matt asked.

Kelley nodded miserably, lit a cigar and waited while Matt put on his hat, then struggled into his sheepskin, leaving the coat unbuttoned. On the cot, Kitty stirred and opened her eyes. "Take care, Matt." Kitty rose from the cot, moved to Matt's side, and squeezed his hand.

The marshal nodded. He opened the door and stumped outside on his crutch, Kelley following close behind. Flurries of snow tumbled along the street, and over at the Long Branch, men's breath clouded the freezing air.

"Let's hear it, Henry!" Matt yelled.

"And be damned to ye," Kelley added.

"Come closer," Henry yelled. "I want you to hear what I have to say real good. I don't need no misunderstandings. Let's make sure like good Christians we're all singing off the same page in the hymn book."

Matt and Kelley stepped off the boardwalk onto the deep, slushy snow in the street, the darkness of the night finally falling behind them. The mayor stuck his cigar in the corner of his mouth and drew the collar of his coat higher around his ears, his eyes on Henry.

When they were halfway across the street, Matt stopped, reached out and grabbed the back of the mayor's coat, pulling him to a halt also.

"I want you closer," Henry said. The third outlaw had split to Henry's right, his rifle held at waist level, pointed at the marshal.

"We can hear you from here," Matt said. "What's on your mind, Henry? Say your piece."

Matt did not want to close the distance. There was always the slender chance he could get a clear shot at Waters. The forty feet or so between them required aimed fire and could nullify the speed of the gunman's draw. And the shifting veil of the falling snow might lessen his accuracy. Once he dropped Waters, Matt could then try for Henry and the other man — if he was still standing. It would be a desperate play and a mighty slim hope, like trying to argue with the angel of death, but right now it was all Matt Dillon had.

If Henry suspected Matt's motive, he obviously dismissed the big lawman's chances, because he now spoke up. "I'll make this real simple so it's easy to understand," he said, the deep, terrible scar on his cheekbone standing out livid white. "I want three things. One, all the money from the other banks in town delivered to me here at the Long Branch. Two, I want Kitty Russell on account of how I'm making her my new woman. Three, that Greenwood heiress gal is to be sent to me here. Later me and her pappy will have us a little talk."

Henry pointed at Kelley. "Mayor, you will see that all these demands are met by noon or the doc hangs." He turned to Waters. "Give him a taste o' the rope, Deke."

Keeping Sam Noonan and another man between him and Matt, the gunman pushed two of his hostages into position behind Doc and made them take hold of the end of the rope. "Swing him up," he said.

The men hesitated, their faces ashen, and Waters' gun flashed into his hand. "Do like I said. Swing him now!"

Suddenly afraid, the two townsmen

hauled on the rope. The pulley squealed and Doc was slowly lifted off his feet. He hung there, legs kicking, his face turning purple, slowly strangling.

Waters waited for a few moments, then said: "That's enough for now. Let him down."

The men released the rope and Doc collapsed in a heap on the boardwalk.

"See? I mean what I say," Henry yelled, his black eyes blazing. "Meet all my demands by noon or the doc dies. And I'll hang one man every hour thereafter until you damn people come to your senses."

Kelley was a shrewd old he-coon from high up the creek and he'd read the signs. "Henry," he said, his voice cracked by urgency and concern, "we'll bring you the money. Take it and ride out of here. Just let those men go and we won't try to stop you."

The outlaw shook his head. "You heard me plain enough, Mayor. I want the money and the women, and I want it all by noon. And one more thing. We're out of grub and wood for the stove. See we get that as well."

Matt had no chance. There were too many men between him and Waters. His hope of getting a clean shot at the gunman was dashed. If he drew now, he'd die uselessly in the street and Scar Henry would have his way with the town and everyone in it — including Kitty.

He watched Henry turn on his heel and walk into the saloon. Waters lingered for a few moments, talking to the outlaw with the rifle. The man lined up the hostage townsmen along the boardwalk, then yanked Doc to his feet. He took the end of the rope, hauled on it until Doc was standing on tiptoe, and tied it off to a bench.

The man then stood with his back to the saloon wall, his Winchester covering the shivering prisoners, and nodded to Waters as the gunman stepped into the Long Branch.

Matt took his watch from his vest and thumbed open the case. It was a few minutes after eight . . . less than four hours until noon.

Chapter 14

Councils of War

As he walked back across Front Street, Matt Dillon made up his mind. He was tired of canned beans. It was time to pay a visit to Ma's Kitchen and eat a decent breakfast.

When he returned to the office, Kitty was up and dressed and he asked her to accompany him. When they came back, Festus could go eat.

"Henry won't make a move until noon," Matt explained. "I reckon we'll be safe until then."

"Do you have a plan, Matthew?" Festus asked, a worried frown wrinkling his forehead.

"I'm still studying on it," the big marshal answered.

"Time's a-runnin' out, Matthew," Festus said, failing to hide his disappointment, pointing out a grim fact that Matt already knew.

The marshal nodded. "I'm aware of that, Festus, and like I said, I'm studying on it. I just haven't thrown my saddle on a good notion yet."

Festus' pointed glance at the clock on the wall was an unspoken comment and Matt smiled inwardly. But his deputy was right. He'd have to make a move soon — and blow this whole situation sky high.

Even without her makeup, Kitty Russell was a stunningly beautiful woman. She had changed into a blue wool dress and had tied her hair back with a ribbon of the same color. Over the dress she wore a cloak of darker blue with a wide hood, high-buttoned boots on her dainty feet.

She and Matt stepped along the icy boardwalk to the restaurant, its windows steamed up, the smell of coffee, frying steak and bacon hanging in a fragrant cloud outside the door.

When Kitty and Matt stepped inside, a few of the town businessmen were eating. They turned and watched the marshal, their eyes filled with anticipation. By now everyone knew of the hostage crisis and Scar Henry's demands, and it seemed to Matt that these men expected him to already be doing something daring and heroic.

Instead, he ordered steak, eggs and biscuits, and he realized by their crestfallen faces and low, whispered conversations that they were sorely disappointed.

Matt dug in with an appetite, but Kitty barely ate, picking at her food. Finally she gave up and settled for coffee.

"Off your feed?" Matt asked.

Kitty nodded. "Matt, I keep thinking about Doc. He's not a young man anymore and they have him standing out in this cold. He could catch pneumonia."

A slight smile tugged at the corners of Matt's mouth. "You're not worried that Scar Henry plans to hang him?"

Kitty's eyes dropped to the cup she held at her lips. "I'm not allowing myself to think about that. It can't happen. I won't let it happen."

"I won't let it happen either, Kitty," Matt said.

Hope flared in Kitty's eyes. "Then you do have a plan!"

The marshal nodded. "I do. But it's going to take a tremendous sacrifice on your part. Kitty, I'm about to ask you to do something that tears me up inside every time I think about it. The only trouble is, I see no other way."

"What is it, Matt?" Kitty asked, her scared eyes on his, fearful about what was to come next.

Matt sighed, laid his knife and fork on his empty plate.

And then he told her.

After the marshal stopped speaking, Kitty sat in silence for a long while, lost in her own thoughts. Her face was strained, pale as she contemplated the unthinkable.

"I've asked too much of you," Matt said, trying to allay Kitty's fears and perhaps offer her a way out. "Maybe some sacrifices are just too great to make."

"Doc's life is at stake," Kitty said, her beautiful face bleak. "I've been sitting here arguing with myself. But I already knew the result of it all would be that I'd do what you ask."

"Are you sure?" Matt said, himself uncertain. "Could be I can find another way."

Kitty shook her head. "Do what you have to do, Matt. There is no other way."

Snow was falling heavier as Kitty and Matt left the restaurant and headed along the boardwalk to the marshal's office. Doc, Sam Noonan and the other prisoners were still lined up outside the Long Branch, shivering, guarded by the outlaw with the rifle.

It was almost nine when Festus left for

the restaurant, promising to be back in thirty minutes.

Matt was worried by his deputy's appearance. Festus was ghostly pale, the dark shadows under his eyes and the hollows of his cheeks deepening. Blood loss from his wounds had weakened him; normally a robust man, he walked with the slow, hesitant gait of an invalid.

Matt needed Festus now more than ever, and he was troubled, knowing he was about to place demands on his deputy the man was physically too weak to handle.

But there was no alternative. Festus would have to step up and play his part. In his favor, Festus was game as they come, ready for anything, possessed of the kind of sand a man needs when he runs out of options.

He'd do. He'd have to.

Since Henry wouldn't make a move until his noon deadline, Matt gambled and left Kitty in his locked office while he sought out Mayor Kelley.

All movement along Front Street was difficult now because of the driving snow. Visibility was down to about ten yards and as Matt stumped his way along the boardwalk, which was treacherous with slush and ice, he could barely make out the figures of the men standing, huddled together, outside the Long Branch.

The mayor's house was at the edge of town, set in open ground. Matt was cold and his leg hurt when he finally stumped onto the porch and knocked on the door.

When Kelley ushered Matt into his parlor, the marshal saw no sign of Isobel Charles-Greenwood, but he heard the woman's voice upstairs, shrill with anger, berating her maid over something or other.

Kelley made the long-suffering face of a martyred saint and made no comment, merely rolling his eyes, as he waved Matt into a chair.

"You look like a man who could use a brandy, Matt," the mayor said. "I have a bottle of Hennessy and it's about time it was opened."

Kelley found the brandy, poured Matt and himself a generous glass, then sat in an overstuffed chair opposite the marshal. "Now what can I do for you?"

After the big lawman told Kelley his plan, the mayor stiffened in shock. "And Miss Kitty is all right with this?"

Matt nodded. "She doesn't like it, but she knows it has to be done."

"She's a remarkable woman, Miss Kitty," Kelley said. He rolled his eyes to the floor upstairs. "I only wish there were more like her."

"Just be ready when the time comes, Mayor," Matt said. "I don't want Kitty's sacrifice to be for nothing."

"Right!" Kelley stood and gleefully rubbed his hands together. "Action at last. Now we'll finally get rid of that Henry scoundrel." He watched as Matt drained his brandy and struggled to his feet. "I'll round up all the men I can and meet you at your office," Kelley said.

"No," Matt said. "Henry or one of the others will be watching and their suspicions will be roused. Have two good riflemen standing somewhere out of sight opposite the Long Branch. You and the others meet Festus and me behind the New York Hat Shop at ten minutes before noon. And, Mayor, for God's sake don't be late or let yourselves be seen."

"We'll be careful, Matt," Kelley said. He hesitated, his shrewd eyes searching the marshal's face, gauging his confidence. "This is a mighty desperate plan. Do you think it will work?"

"It has to work," Matt answered. "If it doesn't, Kitty and all of us will lose."

"You mean we'll end up with all grits and no ham."

Matt nodded. "That's about the size of it, Mayor."

"Then we'll just have to make sure it doesn't fail," Kelley said. "Matt, maybe you should say a prayer to Saint Jude."

"Who's he?"

"The patron saint of lost causes and hopeless cases," the Mayor answered.

"This stuff is old, Marshal," Newly O'Brien said, his mouth tight with concern. "I stocked it for the Santa Fe when they were laying track north of here, but it turned out it wasn't needed and I was stuck with it."

"Newly," Matt said, "tell me one thing — after I light the fuses, will the dynamite go boom?"

"Sure it will. Trouble is, it could go boom before you light the fuses. Like I told you, it's old, and when it's old, it's mighty uncertain. Dynamite is just a paste of gelignite mixed up with sawdust in a paper tube — and gelignite goes up if you even look at it the wrong way."

"Then so be it. I reckon I'll just have to take my chances."

The two men stood in O'Brien's gun store, surrounded by racks of gleaming new Winchesters and glass cases full of the latest revolvers. Fly rods and an assortment of reels hung on the walls, since the gunsmith also catered to fishermen.

"How many sticks to bring the whole back of the building down?" Matt asked.

O'Brien shrugged. "I'd say a couple of sticks ought to do it. Only it won't go down, Marshal. It will go up, high up. Then it will come down — around your head."

"You know how to encourage a man, don't you, Newly?" Matt smiled.

"I just like my customers to know the facts," the gunsmith said, unfazed. "I sell a man a rifle or a fishing rod, I tell him what to expect from it and what not to expect."

Newly disappeared into the back room of the store, and when he returned a few minutes later, he carried two sticks of dynamite, yellowish cylinders eight inches long and an inch in diameter, blasting caps and fuses already in place.

"This stuff is sweating, Marshal," the gunsmith said, his face grim. "I didn't realize it was so bad or I'd have gotten rid of it months ago. Be real careful."

Matt hesitated for a few moments, then said: "Newly, you know what I plan to do. You're the best rifle shot in Dodge and when this thing blows, I'd like you to be opposite the Long Branch with your Winchester."

O'Brien reached behind him, took a rifle from the rack and began to feed shells into the chamber from a box on the counter. "Thought you'd never ask," he said.

When Matt returned to the office, Festus was already there. "Eat something?" the marshal asked.

The deputy shook his head. "I'm plumb off my feed, Matthew. Only had me but one steak an' a half dozen eggs, an' I had to force myself to get that morsel down. Well, that an' some o' Ma's buttermilk biscuits. I brung the prisoner some grub though."

"Festus," Matt said, "we have something to do, and with such a small amount of breakfast in you, I hope you're up for it."

"I'm feelin' right poorly, but I reckon I'm up for it, Matthew," the deputy said. "Tell me what's on your mind."

Matt told Festus about his meetings with Mayor Kelley and Newly O'Brien, and when he finished, he summed it up. "So when the back of the Long Branch goes sky-high, we rush inside shooting and rescue Doc and the rest of the prisoners."

His face stunned into immobility, Festus

turned to Kitty, who was sitting on the edge of the cot. "An' you told Matthew you'd go along with this, Miss Kitty?"

Kitty nodded. "Only a real big diversion will allow you and Matt and the others to get inside the Long Branch before Henry and his men know what's happening." She managed a weak smile. "I'm told a dynamite explosion is a pretty big diversion."

"But . . . but them diamond dust mirrors you had brung all way from Paris, France . . . an' . . . an' the New Orleans roulette wheel . . . an' . . . an' —"

"Festus, those things aren't important," Kitty said. "They're only possessions. If it comes to it, I'd willingly give away everything I own to save the lives of Doc and Sam Noonan and those other men."

Festus let that sink in, then asked: "Matthew, suppose ol' Henry an' them scamper out the front door while we're a-chargin' in the back?"

"Newly and a couple of other good riflemen will be posted across the street. If Henry and Waters decide to make a run for it, they'll hit a blizzard of lead."

Festus slapped his thigh with his one good hand. "Sounds like it could work! I'd like to see ol' Scar's face when the Long Branch blows up around his ears." The deputy's face took on a stricken look. "Oh, Miss Kitty, I'm real sorry."

Kitty smiled. "It's all right, Festus. Truth to tell, I'd like to see that myself."

Chapter 15

Battle at Noon

The snow was falling heavier, but the wind off the plains had dropped and the flakes drifted straight down, drawing a ragged lace curtain across the front of the Long Branch.

When Matt stepped to the window and looked outside, he could just make out Doc and the other prisoners huddled together on the boardwalk, their guard standing back toward the saloon door. There was no sign of Henry or Waters.

Matt nodded, his face set and grim. The absence of those two would mean they were somewhere inside the Long Branch, and if he was real lucky, the planned explosion might kill them both.

But the marshal wasn't counting on it. It seemed that Henry and Waters had more lives than a pair of cats, and they were men who knew how to survive.

The office clock stood at eleven thirty. Matt gloomily contemplated the snow, willing it to stop. Newly O'Brien and the mayor's riflemen needed clear sight pictures if Henry and Waters broke and ran, but the snow obscured everything, and their targets would be fleeting and uncertain.

Well, there was nothing he could do about the weather. He had to act because Heaven never favors the man who hesitates and does nothing.

"Let's go, Festus," Matt said, turning from the window. "I'd say we're going to have us a time."

As his deputy picked up the Greener, Matt buttoned into his coat and settled his hat on his head. He shucked his Colt and shoved it into the right pocket of the coat, where it would be handier. Then he opened the brown paper wrapped around the dynamite sticks. Both were sweating worse than ever, drops of pure gelignite beading the paper tubes.

Festus, as aware of the dangerous condition of the sticks as Matt, raised one eyebrow, showing his concern, but said nothing.

Conscious of a tenseness in the two men, Kitty rose from the edge of the cot. "Matt, be careful," she said, her mouth working, all the unexpressed devotion she felt for this tall, honorable man summed up in those three words.

The big marshal nodded. He tried, but could not find the right thing to say, so he let it go. He wrapped up the dynamite again, found his crutch and stomped to the door. "It's time, Festus," he said.

Matt opened the door and struggled outside, hearing Kitty's soft, sudden sob behind him, the desolate sound a knife to his heart.

As they'd done when they rescued Kitty, Matt and Festus worked their way around the hat shop and then behind the Long Branch. The coats of both men were plastered white with snow and the day was very cold. What wind there was gnawed at their faces with icy teeth.

Their feet crunching, the lawmen took up a position in the deep snow behind the freight wagon. Now it was up to Mayor Kelley.

The effort of struggling through the drifts on his crutch had exhausted Matt, and his breath came in short, sharp gasps, puffs of gray vapor escaping between his tight, grimacing lips as the snow fell around him.

"You all right, Matthew?" Festus whispered, his eyes worried.

Matt nodded. "I'll be fine. Just a

smidgen out of breath, is all." He looked around him. Where the heck was Kelley?

The mayor and a half dozen men, all of them carrying rifles or shotguns, emerged through the curtain of thick snow a few minutes later.

"Did you post men opposite the saloon?" Matt whispered.

"Dan Gaites and Burt Lewis," the mayor answered.

Matt knew Gaites and Lewis. Both were war veterans who were good shots and would stand their ground. "They'll do," he said.

Kelley reached inside his coat and found his watch. "Almost ten until noon," he said, snapping the cover shut. "It's time." He nodded toward the brown paper parcel in Matt's hand. "Is that the dynamite?"

"Two sticks," the marshal answered.

Kelley turned and motioned toward a young man with a sweeping blond mustache. "Ransom here will light the fuses and place them against the back wall," Kelley said. "He's young and he can move fast."

Matt shook his head. "This stuff is dangerously unstable. I'll do it."

Before Kelley could protest, the marshal moved out from behind the wagon and made his way toward the rear wall of the saloon. Snow was piled anywhere from three to ten feet high against the timber boards, and only one spot was relatively clear, the path someone had made from the back door to the outhouse.

The dynamite would have to be placed there, against the door.

Matt didn't know if confining the dynamite to one spot like that would be enough to bring down the whole back wall of the Long Branch. But, the way he figured it, he had no other choice. The high drifting snow had seen to that.

The marshal glanced over his shoulder and was comforted by the fact that Festus, Kelley and the other men were alert and ready, their guns at the high port.

He pushed closer to the door, his crutch sometimes sticking fast in the snow or slipping and sliding, threatening to unbalance him. Now and again, despite the pain it caused him, he was forced to put weight on his broken leg. The sock on his foot was soaked through and he could no longer feel his toes. Ten feet to go. For Matt Dillon a forbidding, endless distance.

He struggled forward. His crutch went deep into the snow and the tip landed on top of a buried bottle or an empty can.

The crutch skidded and went out from under him. Matt stumbled and fell headlong, the dynamite flying out of his hand.

He lay there stunned for a few moments, then became aware of Kelley standing over him. "Matt, are you all right?" the mayor whispered, his voice sharp edged with worry.

"I'm fine," Matt answered, his eyes lifting to the mayor. "Just help me to my feet and then get back behind the wagon."

Kelley, stocky and strong, reached down and pulled on the marshal's arm, yanking him into a standing position. The mayor found the crutch and handed it to Matt. Then the dynamite.

The marshal nodded his thanks. "Now get back with the others, Mayor," he said. "We're running out of time, and timing has plenty to do with the outcome of this rain dance."

Matt covered the remaining distance without incident. He stretched his broken leg out in front of him, got down on his right knee and carefully placed the dynamite sticks upright at each side of the door. With a pang of unease he noted that the fuses looked a whole sight shorter than they done in Newly O'Brien's gun store.

Matt reached into his pocket, found a

match and thumbed it into flame. An errant wind, cartwheeling a flurry of snow, swirled around the corner of the saloon and promptly blew it out.

Cursing under his breath, the icy snow stinging his face, Matt tried again. This time the match was damp and all the big lawman got for his trouble was a red smear across his thumbnail.

How close was it to noon? Too close!

Driven by desperation, Matt found another match. The match flared with a brief whiff of sulfur, and he cupped the bright yellow flame in his left hand.

Slowly, with infinite care, he lit one fuse. It sputtered as the black powder at its thin twine core ignited, throwing off a shower of sparks. Matt reached over to light the second fuse — but the flame burned down one side of the match and died.

Despite the intense cold, sweat beaded the marshal's forehead as he groped around in his pocket for another match. He found it. His last one. Again he thumbed the match into flame and touched it to the second fuse. It sputtered like the first, then began to burn.

Matt struggled to his feet, tucked his crutch under his arm and made his slow, painful way back toward the wagon. He saw an agitated Kelley gesturing at him to hurry. The mayor's mouth was wide open, yelling something Matt could not hear.

The marshal tried to move faster, but the crutch slowed him. Festus came out from behind the wagon and started to plow through the snow toward him. Matt waved the deputy back.

And then the whole world exploded.

The tremendous blast caught Matt in midstride. A gigantic fist crashed into his back, slamming him into the snow. An avalanche of debris — glass, plaster, broken beams, chunks of timber — rained over him in a clattering, shattering shower.

Matt became aware of feet crunching fast through the snow as men passed him. Kelley yelled and guns banged. Then came more gunfire, this time the flat reports of rifles out in the street and the angry staccato bark of revolvers.

Suddenly Festus was at Matt's side. The deputy helped him to his feet and the big marshal turned toward the Long Branch . . . and beheld the utter devastation he had wrought.

The entire back half of the saloon was gone. Through the heavy curtain of the snow Matt could see the bar, or what was left of it, and a tangle of scattered tables and chairs. The diamond dust mirrors were gone, broken into a million pieces, and a dull red fire glowed in a corner, feeding on a pair of velvet drapes. The floorboards were torn up and splintered all the way to the door of the saloon and the huge crystal chandelier that Kitty had brought from Denver hung precariously askew on just one of its chains.

But Matt had no time for regret. He pulled the gun from his pocket and, Festus beside him, struggled through the snow and into the wrecked Long Branch. One of Kelley's men, a white-haired oldster named Micah Lewis, lay sprawled and dead on the floor. Lewis, a former miner, did odd jobs around town and Matt had liked the old man.

The two lawmen made their way to the front of the saloon and onto the boardwalk. Doc and the other prisoners, blue with cold, but unhurt, stood around Mayor Kelley, telling him he'd done good and offering him their profuse thanks. Their outlaw guard was draped across the top of the hitching rail outside, his eyes open but empty, the front of his mackinaw splashed with blood. But where were Henry and Waters?

Matt stomped to the edge of the boardwalk, his eyes searching the snow-shrouded street, looking for the bodies of the two outlaws. He saw nothing, only the lanky figure of Newly O'Brien stepping quickly toward him.

"Did you get them?" Matt yelled when the gunsmith was still yards away.

O'Brien shook his head but made no reply until he reached the boardwalk. A new Winchester hung loose in his right hand and the man's face was bleak. "We didn't nail them, Marshal," he said. "As soon as the saloon went up and Mayor Kelley's men opened fire, Henry and that gunman of his lit out. They crossed the street, right in the open, but the snow was falling so thick we couldn't get a clear shot." O'Brien's face lightened slightly. "But I'm sure I winged Henry. He was limping last I saw him."

Matt shook his head, a bitter disappointment in him. "Henry always limps. He must have taken a bullet in the leg sometime."

Reading the big lawman's face, O'Brien said quickly: "We'll find them. We'll fan out and search the whole town."

"Newly, take a few men and get over to the livery stable. They'll go for their horses and maybe you can stop them there."

O'Brien nodded, called out the names of a couple of men, then led them through the thickly falling snow to the stable.

Kelley stepped beside Matt. "Old Micah Lewis is gone," he said. "That was Waters' doing." The mayor shrugged. "But he was nearly eighty years old. He had a good run."

"Maybe so," Matt answered. "But I reckon he wanted to see another sunrise, just like the rest of us."

He looked in the direction of the livery stable, where O'Brien and his men were already lost in the snow. Matt knew it would be a wild-goose chase. Scar Henry and Deacon Waters were long gone. And letting the cats out of the bag had been a lot easier than putting them back would be.

Chapter 16

Another Checkmate

"They must be around town somewhere, Matt," Mayor Kelley said, scowling his disappointment. "O'Brien says their horses are still at the livery." The two men stood amid the wreckage of the Long Branch, flurries of windblown snow drifting around them.

Kitty, her face composed but her eyes moist, was stepping carefully through debris, picking up a broken beer glass here, a shard of mirror there, examining each piece with keen interest before tossing it away.

Kitty was hurting bad, Matt knew, and he wanted to reach out to her. But that would have to wait. Right now his immediate concern must be to find Henry and Waters.

"Where have your men looked, Mayor?" Matt asked.

"Where? Everywhere! It's like those two killers have vanished into thin air."

"Then call off your search. I don't want your men tangling with Waters — or

Henry, come to that. Festus and me will hunt them down."

"You'll need help, Matt," Kelley said. "Festus is dead on his feet and you're in no better shape with a broken leg. You can't do it alone."

"Call off the search, Mayor." Matt glanced at Kelley, his eyes cold. "If your men meet up with Deacon Waters, we'll be storing a lot more bodies until spring. Finding those outlaws is a job for the law, and in this town, Festus and me are the law."

"Then have it your own way," Kelley said shortly. "But when you come looking for my help, Marshal, remember to eat crow while it's still warm. The colder it gets, the harder it is to swallow."

Before Matt could answer, the mayor turned on his heel and stomped out of the saloon, the back of his neck an angry red.

Festus was standing off a ways, and now he cast Matt a look before his eyes, holding an unspoken question, slanted to Kitty.

The marshal nodded, and as Festus slipped out of the saloon, he stepped next to the silent woman. "Kitty," he whispered, "I just don't have the words."

Kitty turned and looked up at Matt, her eyes brimming. "Just hold me, Matt. Hold me for a very long time."

Aware that time was passing quickly, Matt nevertheless took Kitty in his arms and held her close. They stood like that for several minutes, saying nothing as the snow danced around them and the uncaring, teasing wind billowed and tugged at Kitty's cloak.

But then it was time to leave.

Matt let Kitty go and held her at arm's length. He smiled and said: "I have to go. Festus and me, we have things to do."

Kitty nodded, dropping her eyes from his. When she raised them again, there was a gleam of defiance in her look. "I'll rebuild, Matt. I'll return the Long Branch to what it was, just as though nothing had ever changed."

"I know you will, Kitty," Matt said. "And I'll do everything in my power to help you."

Kitty opened her mouth to speak, but Festus' urgent call from the door stopped her.

"Matthew! I reckon you'd better come see this."

The marshal thumped to the door and stepped onto the boardwalk. He followed Festus' nod to farther down Front Street, where Mayor Kelley, hatless, his thin hair plastered wetly to his head, was slowly trudging toward them.

As the man got closer, Matt saw that his face was a stricken gray, his eyes wide and shocked as he stared numbly ahead.

Kelley stumbled and shuffled onward, the snow and the deepening day falling around him. When he reached the boardwalk he looked up at Matt and said, his words sounding flat, like rocks dropping into a tin bucket: "I know where Scar Henry is, Marshal. He's at my house."

"Sometimes you get, and sometimes you get got, and we got got," Kelley said.

The mayor was sitting in Matt's chair at the marshal's office, a steaming cup of coffee sitting, untouched, on the desk in front of him.

"Mayor, tell us what happened," Festus urged, "but in sight plainer American than that."

"You want it plain?" Kelley asked, some of his old belligerence returning. "Then here it is, plain as I can tell it. Scar Henry has my wife and Isobel Charles-Greenwood." The mayor picked up the hot tin cup by the rim, studied it for a few moments, then laid it down again. "After the Long Branch blew, they doubled back and ran straight to my house," he said. "How they knew it was mine, I don't know, unless one of the men they were holding prisoner told them."

Matt nodded. "That seems likely. I guess somebody was trying to save his own neck."

"Well, they were laying for me when I got back. Henry's gunman, Waters, had the muzzle of his revolver pressed against my wife's head, and he was just standing there, grinning, telling me if I made a move for my gun he'd scatter that sainted woman's brains."

"What does Henry want?" Matt asked.

"Want? He wants all the things he wanted before. Jesus, Mary and Joseph and all the saints in Heaven, Matt, don't you see? Nothing has changed. We're right back to where we started."

"So Henry made the same demands," Matt said, his voice cold and angry. "What else did he tell you?"

Kelley shrugged, a dejected picture of misery. "He says he and Waters plan to ride out of here just as soon as the snow lifts and maybe before. Henry wants all the money in town and he aims to keep Mrs. Charles-Greenwood." The mayor's bleak eyes lifted to Matt's. "And he wants Miss Kitty."

"And if we refuse?"

"He says we have two days or less if the weather breaks. And if we refuse, he says he'll shoot my wife."

"Sure laid it on the line again, didn't he?" Festus said.

Matt nodded, thinking about Rose Kelley, a plump, laughing Irishwoman with a heart of gold and a generous soul. "The mayor is right," he said finally. "We're right back to where we started."

"Marshal," Kelley said, "I don't want anything to happen to my missus. And I don't want anything to happen to Mrs. Charles-Greenwood either."

Matt shrugged. "She's not a citizen of Dodge City. My main concern is about your wife."

Kelley erupted. "Think, man! Barton Charles is a man of enormous wealth, and that gives him tremendous power and influence. He also happens to be a major shareholder of the Santa Fe Railroad. If anything happened to his daughter in Dodge, he could get his revenge by rerouting the rails to some other town and leave us to wither on the vine. He could destroy us, Matt — this town, you, me, everyone in it. Without the spring herds, Dodge would be nothing, just another sleepy, jerkwater burg slowly fading away into the prairie."

Kelley leaned forward, tried his coffee and grimaced. "This is even worse than usual." He raised his eyes to Matt, the new and dangerous situation standing like an invisible wall between them. "You're aware of the problem we face. So do you have a plan?"

Matt shook his head. "No, I don't." The big lawman managed a weak smile. "We can't blow up your house, not with your wife and the other woman there."

"Two sticks of dynamite," Kelley said bitterly. "The best saloon in town destroyed, and it got us nowhere."

"We saved Doc's life an' Sam Noonan an' all them other fellers," Festus pointed out mildly.

"Right, we did," the mayor said. "Now you two figure out how to save the lives of my wife and Mrs. Charles-Greenwood."

Chapter 17

The Widow's Grief

The day was shading into night when Matt left the marshal's office. Despite the gathering darkness, he had three places to go and his first stop was the telegraph office.

"Still down, Marshal," Barney Danches said. "Key's been quiet for days."

"You've tried getting out, Barney?" Matt asked.

The agent nodded. "Sure have. Watch this."

Danches sat at his desk and tapped on the telegraph key, a long string of chattering code that made no sense to Matt.

The agent stopped and sat back, waiting. There was no response. "Yup, still down." Danches shook his head. "Could be days before it's back up and running."

Disappointment tugged at Matt. He had a half-formed and vague idea of summoning help from the other lawmen down the line. He doubted that the marshal could have done anything to resolve the situation, but the very presence of a few more tin stars in Dodge might have given Henry and Waters pause and caused them to change their plans.

It had been a slender hope to begin with, but like a drowning man, Matt was clutching at straws, and now one of them had just been snatched away from him.

"Barney, if the key starts up again, come let me know right away," he said.

"Sure will, Marshal," Danches said. The man hesitated, then asked: "What's going to become of us, Matt? Are those bandits going to ride roughshod over the whole town until we're stripped bare of everything we own?" Danches shook his head, his face suddenly lumpy and old. "All my savings were in the Cattleman's Bank, every penny. I was counting on that money for my retirement. I figured I'd buy me a cabin in a place where it never snows — Texas maybe. Planned to sit on my front porch with a cup of coffee of an evening and watch the sun go down." Danches' eyes lifted to Matt's. "That's what I planned."

The big marshal smiled and placed his hand on the agent's thin shoulder. "You'll get your cabin, Barney. Scar Henry isn't leaving here with the town's money in his saddlebags. Depend on it."

Then, deciding to give the anguished man something, Matt added: "You've lived a good, honorable life, Barney. When you're sitting on your porch in Texas, watching the sun go down, you'll be able to think back on it and enjoy it all a second time. Trust me. That's how it's going to happen."

Danches nodded. "Thank you, Marshal. Thank you for at least holding out the hope."

As the day died around him, Matt made his slow, painful way to the rail depot. The news there was no better. The agent had not been able to use his telegraph either, and he had no idea when the next train might arrive.

"Maybe a week," John Quigley said. "Maybe longer. It all depends on the weather."

The man looked at the marshal, wanting to talk, a question in his eyes. But Matt headed him off by stepping to the door of the office. "If you hear anything, let me know," he said.

Now he had to see Jane Morgan, a task that filled him with unease. By rights, Mayor Kelley should have spoken to the widow, but he had made no move in that direction. Matt had decided to take the job on himself, and try to reassure the grieving woman that her husband's killers would be brought to justice.

Perhaps his visit would lift her out of her lethargy and start her on the path to life again.

As Matt struggled through snow and the growing cold, he felt it was worth a try . . . or was he clutching at yet another straw that might soon be snatched away from him?

The Morgan home was a modest wood-frame house situated just over the tracks, well away from its bigger, richer neighbors. Even by Dodge City standards, the house was small, no bigger than a two-room cabin, the kind of home a lowly bank clerk could afford.

But someone, probably Jane herself, had made an effort to transform the house into something better than it was. The house was painted white, with a bright blue door, and there was a small porch out front. Window boxes, now empty of flowers, would add a bright splash of color in spring and when Matt stomped onto the porch, he noticed that both the door's brass door handle and knocker were brightly polished.

Jane Morgan had obviously been a

house-proud, apple-turnover kind of woman and had done her best to provide a comfortable haven for her husband and children.

Matt knuckled the door, and after a few moments, it swung open. Jed Owens' wife, Martha, a large, buxom woman with graying hair and a kindly, open face, stood in the entrance.

"Oh, it's you, Marshal," she said. "Have you come to see poor Mrs. Morgan?"

Matt nodded. "How is she?"

Martha shook her head. "Not well, not well at all. You'll find out for yourself."

The banker's wife led Matt down a small, narrow hallway and opened the door at the end. "She's inside, Marshal. But I don't know if she'll recognize you or even know you're here."

His hat in his hands, Matt stomped into the room. It was a small, sparsely furnished parlor with a cloth-covered table, a few chairs and an old scarred piano set against one wall. A log burned in the fireplace, shedding the only light into the room since the curtains were closed and the oil lamps were unlit.

When Matt's eyes became accustomed to the gloom, he saw Jane Morgan sitting at the table, an untouched cup of coffee that had long since gone cold sitting in front of her. The woman's unkempt hair fell around her shoulders, though someone, probably Mrs. Owens, had made an attempt to brush it. Even in the shifting, uncertain firelight, Matt saw that Jane Morgan's small, homely face was deathly pale, her eyes wide open, staring into nothing.

The big marshal coughed, but Jane did not look at him. "Mrs. Morgan," he tried again, "Matt Dillon. I thought I'd stop by and see how you were and ask if there is anything you need."

The woman made no answer. From some other room in the house, Matt heard the raised voices of children and Martha Owens gently chiding them for something or other.

Matt took a step closer to the table. "Mrs. Morgan, mind if I sit down?" he asked.

Again the woman did not answer, still staring fixedly ahead. Matt found a chair and sat, propping his crutch against the table.

"I'm sorry about what happened to Silas," he said. "I took it hard."

It was as though Jane Morgan had not heard. Her expression did not change, her white face like stone, a woman whose grief had gone beyond grief and into some form of remote, twilight madness.

Matt, feeling huge and awkward in the tiny parlor, took Jane's small hand in his. The woman's hand was even whiter than her face and it felt cold as ice.

"Mrs. Morgan," he said, "I can't find the words." He hesitated, thinking it through, then tried the best way he knew how. "I know this isn't much consolation for the death of your husband, but the men who murdered Silas won't escape. I plan to see them brought to justice and hanged." Matt sought the woman's eyes in the flickering, orange-streaked darkness. "Do you understand what I'm saying to you?"

There was no response. Jane Morgan continued to stare with dead eyes into a space just in front of her. She had gone to a place that was far beyond his reach and Matt felt a sudden sense of defeat.

He rose to his feet and found his crutch. "I'll be back to see you," he said, knowing his words were only a polite fiction. "After it's over."

The big marshal waited for a few moments, hoping for a reaction. There was none.

He stepped to the door, careful of his crutch in the gloom. Then he stopped when behind him he heard what sounded like a low, animal growl.

He turned quickly and saw Jane Morgan looking at him, her face a grotesque, twisted mask of hate. "Kill them, Marshal," she spat, hissing like an enraged cat. "Kill every last one of them and let me dance on their graves."

Matt opened his mouth to speak, but stopped. Jane had turned away from him and was again staring into nothingness, slipping away to that cold gray place where his words could not reach her.

The woman's contorted, hate-filled face still burning on his consciousness, Matt stepped out of the room and closed the door quietly behind him.

Martha Owens met him in the hallway, hurrying past with a .44.40 Winchester she held by the top of the barrel. "This was Silas' hunting rifle," the woman explained. "I'm hiding it from Jane. In her present state of mind, she could use it to . . . to harm herself."

Martha's eyes lifted to the tall lawman. "Did you talk to her?" she asked.

Matt nodded. "I tried."

"Did it do any good?"

"It did no good at all," Matt said. "In fact, maybe I made things worse."

* * *

"I've lost my appetite," Matt said, dropping his tin fork into the can of beans in his hand, his visit with Jane Morgan still very much on his mind. "Or maybe I've just had enough of beans."

"We used to have a saying in the Rangers about our grub," Festus said, eagerly taking Matt's can from him and digging in. "We always said to take a good look at what you eat, not to know what it is, but to know what it was." The deputy nodded, chewing thoughtfully. "In my time I've et most kinds of critters and varmints: coons, possums, prairie dogs an' bobcat a time or two. But I was always right partial to rattlesnake. If'n you cook a snake jes' right, it tastes a lot like fried chicken."

"Thank you, Festus," Kitty said from the edge of the cot. "That makes these beans taste a lot better."

" 'Course mountain lion is good, an' so is alligator, if'n you catch one young enough," Festus continued as though he hadn't heard. "But I say a man's best bet every time is snake."

"Festus sometimes you talk too much," Matt said, smiling. "Now hush up about snakes and critters and leave Kitty to finish her beans in peace."

"I'm finished anyway," Kitty said. She rose and handed what was left of her can to Festus, who took it gratefully. "Well, anyhow, Miss Kitty," he said, "if'n you ever want to know more about critter cookin', all you need do is jes' ask."

"I'll remember that," Kitty said, slanting Matt an amused look. "I really will."

A restlessness riding him, Matt rose and stepped to the window. The snow was still falling and with it the darkness. The wooden buildings along Front Street, their timbers sheeted in thin ice, seemed to be crowding closer together, shouldering each other aside, struggling in a deep silence. The town was locked tight as a drum and the big marshal suddenly found it hard to breathe, like a man being buried alive in a pinched pine coffin.

He needed to do something, find some method of striking at Henry and Waters without endangering the lives of the two women.

There had to be a way.

Chapter 18

Gunfire in the Night

Matt remained awake while Kitty slept on the cot and Festus lay sprawled and snoring on a bunk in the cell next to the silent and sullen outlaw Danny Gannon.

Outside the night lay heavy on Dodge. On Front Street, slanting black shadows tattooed the white skin of the virgin snow, and from somewhere close to town, the coyotes were calling, lingering too long like unloved guests.

The big marshal glanced at the clock on the wall. It was almost nine. A few months from now, when the herds arrived, the town would be shaking itself awake at this time, getting ready to paint its face and whoop it up. But now, in the grip of winter, Dodge was hibernating like a great shambling, shabby bear.

Restlessly, driven by forces he could barely understand, Matt stumped over to the coatrack and shrugged into his sheepskin. He settled his hat on his head, then slipped his Colt into a pocket.

That done, he lowered the flame of the oil lamp above his desk, immediately casting the office into soft amber light.

He had no real plan, no set course of action. Just a vague idea.

It was obvious that Rose Kelley was Scar Henry's bargaining chip. He was using the mayor's wife as he'd done with Doc and the others. She was his guarantee of a safe ticket out of Dodge. Remove Rose from his scheme and Henry would lose much of his bargaining power.

Of course, Isobel Charles-Greenwood was a major consideration. But she was money on the hoof as far as Henry was concerned, and Matt doubted that the outlaw would do anything to harm the woman — at least until after her father had delivered her ransom.

Matt was gambling that he could get Rose Kelley out of Henry's clutches — and that he could do it tonight.

Carefully the marshal eased out of the office and closed the door quietly behind him.

He made his way down the boardwalk in the direction of the Kelley house. The falling snow gave a pale violet cast to the darkness, but the sky was black, without stars. There was no one on the street and all the saloons were closed and shuttered, as though in mourning for the death of the Long Branch.

Matt made his way past Ma's Kitchen, Wilson's hardware store, then the dark Alhambra Saloon. He stepped off the boardwalk when it ended and plowed through knee-deep snow at the junction of Front and Texas streets, almost losing his footing a couple of times.

He regained the icy boardwalk and stomped past several stores, a couple of boarded-up dance halls and another shuttered saloon, the snow caught up by a rising wind driving hard against him.

The boardwalk ended at the last of the commercial buildings, and ahead of him, he saw the lights of a few scattered houses, the homes of bartenders and the like who were not welcome in the lace-curtain side of town.

One of those houses belonged to Mayor Kelley, the earthy Irishman preferring the noise and excitement north of the Deadline to the polite tea and tattle society across the tracks.

The mayor's house, a low white building with a wide front porch, was set well aside from the rest. Kelley had bought it from a reclusive, retired lawyer with no love for people; the house was at least fifty yards from its closest neighbor.

But for the glow of windows and the rectangles of orange splashed on the snow below them, this part of town was wrapped in darkness. Now and again a shadow passed across the angular patches of light but Matt heard no sound, only his own breathing and the soft song of the wind.

The big marshal left the boardwalk and struggled across deep snow toward the Kelley house. At the back of the building was a small barn, where the mayor kept his horse and the Morgan mare that pulled his wife's surrey. The kitchen window at the back of the home looked out across twenty yards of open ground to the barn — and that was where Matt planned to be. From there he could watch the house, and especially the kitchen. Rose Kelley was a woman who loved to cook and eat what she cooked, and Matt was convinced that sooner or later Henry would send her into the kitchen to fix grub or coffee.

As to when that might be, he had no idea. Certainly Henry and Waters would take turns standing guard, and a man needed coffee if he planned to stay awake through the morning hours.

Matt realized fully that the chances of

him pulling off what he had in mind were slim to none, and slim was already saddling up to leave town. But even trying to buck this particular stacked deck was better than sitting in his office doing nothing.

He angled in the direction of the barn, crossing open ground that made him feel exposed and vulnerable. A light glowed in the parlor of the Kelley home, but the rest of the house was in darkness and nothing showed at the windows.

Walking carefully, each step of the way setting his crutch into the snow with care, Matt reached the barn without being seen. He opened the left side of the door and cursed silently as the rusty hinges screeched in protest. Didn't Kelley own an oilcan!

The marshal glanced behind him, but the kitchen was still in darkness. He slipped inside the barn and breathed a sigh of relief. The barn had been built snug and tight, and away from the wind and driving snow, it even felt reasonably warm.

Matt closed the door but cracked it a little so he could keep an eye on the kitchen. Now all he could do was wait . . . and hope.

A slow, silent hour dragged by, the only sound the occasional snort or stomp from the horse stalls and the restless rustle of the searching wind. The snow was still falling steadily and the night had grown colder, and Matt's breath smoked as he shivered and pulled the sheepskin collar of his coat around his ears. He shoved his gun hand deep in his pocket. If the ball opened and shooting started, he didn't want to be stuck with a numb trigger finger.

Ten more minutes slipped past. . . .

It wasn't going to happen, not tonight, Matt thought gloomily. Maybe Henry and Waters weren't coffee-drinking men and maybe they weren't hungry because they'd eaten earlier. The kitchen remained cloaked in darkness and Matt felt his spirits sink even lower. He'd give it another half hour. Then he'd call it a night.

Five minutes later an oil lamp flared in the kitchen. Matt was suddenly alert, his eyes straining to see through the shifting curtain of the snow. Rose Kelley walked past the window, a coffeepot in her hand, then stepped the other way before vanishing from sight. He had his chance — it was now or never.

Carefully the big marshal eased open the creaking barn door. He tucked his crutch under his arm and hobbled as fast as he could toward the kitchen. If Henry or Waters happened to glance out now . . .

He made it to the house and crouched under the window, pale orange light shining on his shoulders and the top of his hat. Matt rose until his eyes were level with the bottom of the window and looked inside. Her back to him, Rose Kelley stood near her glowing stove, busying herself with a small red coffee grinder. There was no one else in the room.

Matt tapped on the window. Too softly. Rose Kelley didn't hear. He tried again, harder this time. The woman turned and her eyes widened when she saw the marshal, her hand flying to her mouth.

Matt beckoned the woman over and pushed up on the window. Like Kitty's window at the Long Branch, this one was also stuck with ice and frost. The marshal tried again, pushing upward with the heels of his hands. It was no good, the window wouldn't budge.

Rose Kelley, her blue eyes bright with fear and alarm, hurried to the stove and returned with the steaming coffeepot. She poured the scalding water around the frame until the pot was empty, looked fearfully over her shoulder and motioned to Matt to try again.

This time when he pushed, the window

slid open easily. "Climb out," Matt told the woman. "Quick!"

Rose hesitated. She was a large, wide-hipped woman and the window was narrow, maybe too narrow.

"Go!" Matt whispered harshly. "We don't have much time."

Her decision made, Rose dived through the window. Her upper half got through, but her hefty hips were stuck fast, her short, tubby legs kicking. Desperately, Matt got hold of the woman's shoulders and pulled. Nothing. He tried again. Rose didn't budge. "Wait, Marshal," the woman whispered. She shifted a little to her right, giving her hips more room. "Now haul away."

Matt pulled, and this time Rose's thickset body jerked free of the window frame. She landed on top of Matt and both went down into the snow in a tangle of arms and legs.

A shout sounded from somewhere in the house. It was Henry's voice, demanding to know what was happening with his coffee.

Rose scrambled to her feet and offered Matt a hand. An immensely strong woman, she lifted his 250 pounds from the ground with ease.

"Go," Matt yelled at her, his need for silence gone. "Run all the way to my office."

Rose hesitated for only a second, saw the urgency in Matt's eyes and ran, her skirt lifted, stubby legs plowing swiftly through the snow.

Matt pulled his gun from his pocket and backed away from the house, into the surrounding darkness. Henry stamped into the kitchen and shouted: "What the hell!"

The outlaw appeared at the window and Matt blasted off a fast shot. The glass shattered and Henry ducked back, cursing.

As Matt backed away, slowed by his crutch and the deep snow, Henry appeared at the window again. The outlaw snapped off two fast shots blindly into the darkness.

Matt fired and saw his shot chip wood from the window frame near Henry's head. The outlaw cursed, louder this time, and shot at the flare of Matt's gun. But the marshal had already sidestepped and Henry missed, his bullet tugging at Matt's sleeve.

Matt fired again, then a second time. His hammering shots shattered more of the glass in the kitchen window and Henry disappeared. Matt doubted that he'd hit the outlaw. The darkness and falling snow made accurate shooting impossible.

The marshal was halfway to the boardwalk when a man, he guessed it was Waters, ran onto the Kelley porch and cut loose with two guns. But the gunman was also firing into snow and darkness, and though his bullets split the air around Matt's head, none came dangerously close.

"Where the hell is he?" Henry yelled. "Did you get him?"

"I don't know," Waters called back. "He sure ain't shooting no more."

The thickening gloom was now Matt Dillon's friend and he held his fire, not wanting to reveal his position to the deadly Waters. He reached the boardwalk as a couple more of the gunman's wild bullets probed the darkness. Matt quickly stomped away, his crutch thumping on the pine boards, and was soon swallowed by the snow and the night.

Chapter 19

A Desperate Encounter

When Matt got back to the office, Kitty and Festus were awake, and Rose Kelley was telling them that she was "scared out of her very wits and all a-tremble."

The big marshal reloaded his Colt and laid it on the table. Then he took off his coat and hat and stepped to the coffeepot on the stove.

"You git any of them, Matthew?" Festus asked, his eyes hopeful.

Matt shook his head. "I doubt it. It was hard to see out there."

"Those terrible men," Rose said, dabbing at her eyes with a small lace handkerchief. "They plan to hold poor Mrs. Charles-Greenwood for ransom. I heard Henry say that her father is the richest man in America and that he'd pay plenty."

Before Matt could comment, the door slammed open and Mayor Kelley stomped inside. "Marshal," he began, "what was all that shooting —"

Rose ran toward him and Kelley's face

showed a combination of shock, surprise and disbelief. "Rosie, me darling, is it really you?"

Mrs. Kelley ran into her husband's arms, sobbing. "As ever was, my love."

Kelley held his wife close, Rose at least twice his size. "But how . . . I mean . . ."

"It was all Marshal Dillon's doing," Rose said. "He rescued me from those awful outlaws."

Kelley led his wife to Matt's chair and bade her sit. "After you compose yourself my dear, we'll go to the Dodge House. I've rented a room there and I have a shotgun close to hand."

"James, you're the very soul of goodness," Rose said, lifting tearstained eyes to her husband. "I must confess it's good to sit down. I'm all a-tremble. I really am."

"What happened, Matt?" Kelley asked.

After the marshal recounted the events of the night, the mayor stuck out his hand and Matt took it. "Thank you for rescuing my wife. It was well done."

"I got lucky." Matt smiled. "For a while there, I reckoned it was a mighty close run thing."

Kelly dropped his hand. "Where do we go from here? Henry still has Mrs. Charles-Greenwood and I fear he means to do her harm if we try to intervene."

"He does," Rose said. "He told the poor young woman that if anyone tries to rescue her, he'll shoot her. And then he said that if her father doesn't come up with a ransom he'll keep her for a while, then sell her to a brothel keeper down on the border." Rose dabbed her eyes again. "He's a terrible, sinful man."

"What should we do, Matt?" Kelley asked.

"We sit tight," the marshal answered. "Henry is bound to make a mistake sooner or later, and when he does, I'll be ready."

"Then let's hope it's sooner rather than later," Kelley said. "We can't let this thing go on and on."

"James," Rose said to her husband, "no one knows better than yourself that I have the gift, and what I feel tonight is making me quite undone."

"My wife has the gift of second sight, sometimes a boon, but more often a thorn in the side of the Irishwoman," Kelley told the others by way of explanation. "She sees things before they happen."

"And what I see is this situation getting a lot worse before it gets better." Rose shook her head, her eyes haunted. "If it ever does get better."

"Come, my dear, it's time to see you safely in bed," Kelley said. The mayor took off his coat and when his wife got to her feet he draped it around her shoulders. "You'll catch your death of cold out there in the snow, and you wearing only a house dress."

Kitty, an impulsive, softhearted woman kissed Rose on the cheek. "Everything will be just fine, Mrs. Kelley," she said. "I know it will."

"Oh, I hope so my dear," Rose said, patting Kitty's hand. "There's been enough shooting and killing in this town. We surely don't need any more."

After the Kelleys left, Festus returned to his bunk and Kitty placed her hand on Matt's shoulder. "You should sleep for a while too. You look tired."

The big marshal nodded. "I reckon I will. It's been a long night."

"Take the cot," Kitty said. "I'll be just fine in your chair."

Matt opened his mouth to object, but a loud call from outside stopped him. "You in the jail!"

The marshal picked up his gun, got his crutch and stomped to the door. He opened it a crack and yelled: "What do you want, Henry?"

"That was ill done, Dillon. A bad night's work. I had thoughts of letting you live, but now I aim to gun you for sure."

"You're welcome to try, Scar. Step out into the street and we'll settle it right now."

Matt's eyes probed the darkness, trying to locate the outlaw. But all he saw through the falling snow was the black silhouettes of the buildings across the street and the dark, angled shadows in the alleys.

"I'll choose my time, Dillon," Henry yelled. "But keep this in mind — as of this night, you're a walking dead man."

When Matt woke, it was already light. At Kitty's insistence he'd slept on the cot. He looked across the office and saw her dozing in his chair, a blanket pulled up to her chin.

The marshal glanced at the clock. It was almost eight. He rose, found his crutch, and shivered as he fed wood into the stove and put the coffee on to boil.

Outside the snow was still falling and the prairie wind had picked up, scattering white flakes along the length of Front Street. Across the way, the Long Branch, a tangle of splintered timbers and shattered beams, tilted at a crazy angle on its foundations. The saloon was wide-open to the snow and wind since the entire back of the building was gone and the roof had been blown off most of the upstairs rooms.

Matt felt a pang of regret, even though the dynamite that had destroyed the Long Branch had accomplished something. Doc and the other men were free. But the terrible cost to Kitty had brought the big lawman no closer to ending the standoff with Henry and Waters, and that failure nagged at him.

"How did you sleep?" Kitty asked, waking suddenly.

"Like a dead calf." Matt smiled. "And you?"

"Just fine. This chair is surprisingly comfortable once you get used to it." She paused. "Of course, it takes a lot of getting used to."

Festus appeared at the door, looking haggard and tired. A patch of brown blood showed on the bandage at his shoulder and he walked with the hesitant step of an old man. "Coffee ready?" he asked. "An' the prisoner will want some."

"Soon," Matt answered. He felt a pang of sympathy for his deputy. "How are you feeling, old-timer?"

"Oh, fair to middlin', Matthew," Festus answered. "But bullet holes have a way of wearin' on a man."

The deputy perched on the corner of the desk. "I mind one time down on the Brazos when I took a Comanch bullet in the leg. Laid me up for near three months and made me feel right peaked the whole time."

"Bullets will do that to you," Matt said, smiling. "I guess that's why they call it coming down with a dose of lead poisoning."

Festus nodded. "That's a natural fact, Matthew. Truer words was never spoke, because about right now I feel like a pizened pup."

The deputy poured coffee into a tin cup for Danny Gannon and slid his Colt from his holster hanging on the gun rack, holding both awkwardly in his left hand. He yawned and said: "I'll be right back."

"Need some help?" Matt asked.

Festus shook his head. "Nah, Gannon's asleep. I can handle it."

Matt poured himself and Kitty coffee, then stepped to the window and looked outside. The night had shaded into a gray dawn and the shadows were slowly being washed from the alleys across the street. The snow was still falling, driven by an icy wind, and Matt was glad of the warmth of the stove, glowing cherry red in the corner.

He turned, just as the door from the cells crashed open and Danny Gannon stood in the doorway, a wild look on his face and Festus' gun in his hand.

Matt heard Kitty's startled intake of breath. Then Gannon said: "Dillon, you killed my brother and now I aim to kill you."

"What did you do to Festus?" Kitty asked, alarm edging her voice.

Gannon grinned. "He's asleep. I gave him what they call a sedative — my fist to his jaw." The outlaw turned all his attention on the big marshal. "How does it feel to be on your feet, Dillon, but already dead? Huh? How does it feel? Do you fear your own death like my brother must have done after you shot him and he coughed up his life blood onto the damn snow?"

If his years had taught Matt Dillon anything, it was that there was a time for talking and a time for doing. Gannon expected him to talk, maybe beg for his life, and the outlaw wanted to draw it out, see the marshal crawl. The man was dangerous and he'd be fast and very accurate with the gun in his fist. His eyes were reckless, his body tense and ready to go, and Matt knew his life was now measured in seconds.

The table to the side of his desk was

small, just big enough for a couple of people to sit. His fully loaded Colt lay on its scarred surface — if he could just get to it.

Matt moved. He suddenly shifted all his weight to his good leg and threw his crutch at Gannon with his left hand. It was an underhand throw and it did not have much power, but it startled the outlaw. The man took a single step back as the crutch bounced off his chest, his gun muzzle coming up. Too high. He triggered a shot but it splintered harmlessly into the timber ceiling.

Matt dived for the table. He landed on its round top, the spindly legs collapsed under his weight and he crashed heavily to the floor. Pain shot through the broken bones in his leg, but he ignored it and reached for the Colt, which had skittered three feet away from him.

The marshal heard Kitty scream as Gannon fired again. Something stung wickedly on Matt's cheek but the gun was in his hand and now instinct took over. Lying on his right side, he raised the gun and fired. Gannon reeled under the impact of the bullet that smashed into him, but he was gamely trying to level his Colt. Matt fired again. The outlaw went up on his toes and his back slammed hard against the wall, shaking the entire office. Gannon triggered a shot, but his bullet went wild. Matt fired again, once, twice. The outlaw slumped against the wall, then slid to his knees. Gannon remained there for a few moments, his eyes wide, staring at Matt in shocked disbelief. But then his fixed stare glazed in death and he saw no more. The gun dropped from Gannon's hand and thudded onto the timber floorboards. He fell flat on his face.

The big marshal grabbed the corner of his desk and pulled himself up until he was standing on his good leg. He sat on the edge of the desk as Kitty rushed to his side. "Matt," she exclaimed, her face stricken, "you've been wounded."

Matt wiped away blood from his cheek with the back of his gun hand and glanced at the crimson smear it left on his skin. "It's a scratch," he said. "His bullet just burned me."

Kitty looked down at the outlaw's body. "Is he . . . is he . . . ?"

"Dead? Yes, about as dead as he's ever going to be." The big marshal slowly shook his head. "He was right. He should never have left Texas."

Chapter 20

Buffalo Soldiers

Percy Crump later added Danny Gannon's body to the growing number of gunshot corpses he had stacked waiting for the spring thaw in his morgue.

Festus, the expression on his face a mix of guilt and dejection, was being fussed over by Kitty, who held snow to the swollen lump on his jaw.

"Matthew, I'm plumb sorry," the deputy said finally, unnerved by the marshal's silence on the matter. "I should never have let Gannon get the drop on me thataway."

Pretending a sternness he didn't feel, Matt scowled and asked: "How did it happen?"

Festus squirmed in his chair and answered: "Well, I thought ol' Danny was sound asleep. He was lyin' on his back a-snorin' like a saw runnin' through a pine tree. I bent over and laid the cup by his cot, plannin' to wake him up, but then his fist shot out and hit me smack on the jaw.

He hit me real good an' then all the lights went out."

Matt laughed and Festus raised his eyes to him in annoyance. "It wasn't funny, Matthew."

"No, it wasn't funny," the big marshal admitted. Now he offered his deputy a way of saving face. "I was just thinking that if you'd been feeling yourself, I mean well and all, a two-bit outlaw like Danny Gannon would never have bushwhacked you like he did."

"He wouldn't?" Festus asked, surprised. Then realizing his slip, he added quickly: "You're right, Matthew — darn tootin' he wouldn't. I'd never have fallen for an old trick like that."

"You sure wouldn't, old-timer." Matt smiled. "Not if you were feeling up to scratch."

Festus nodded. "I jes' wasn't feelin' up to scratch, Matthew."

"That surely was the trouble," Matt said.

The deputy's relieved eyes slid over Matt's shoulder to the window. "So'jers outside."

Six black troopers, wrapped in fur coats and hats, sat their horses at the hitching rail. A white man, dressed in the same manner and showing no signs of rank, swung from the saddle and stepped onto the boardwalk.

Matt let the soldier inside, a tall, slender young man sporting the sweeping dragoon mustache then fashionable among the cavalry officers of the frontier army.

"Lieutenant John Greenwood," the officer said, touching his hat to Kitty. "I'm making inquiries about my wife, Mrs. Isobel Charles-Greenwood." The young officer slapped snow from his coat, his face showing both exhaustion and worry. "She's three days overdue at the fort, and since the telegraph is down, my colonel gave me permission to look for her."

"Your wife is here in Dodge, Lieutenant," Matt said. "And, for the time being at least, she's safe."

Alarm flared in Greenwood's eyes. "For the time being? What does that mean?"

"Maybe you'd better sit down," Matt said.

The officer shook his head. "I'll hear what you have to say standing up." His eyes moved to the star on Matt's vest, and he added: "Marshal."

"Then so be it," Matt said.

Quickly, covering the basic points, the big lawman told Greenwood about the arrival of Scar Henry, the rescue of the soldier's wife from the stalled train and her subsequent capture by Henry and Deacon Waters.

"Henry means to hold your wife for ransom," Matt finished. "I understand her father is a very wealthy man."

Greenwood looked stunned. He nodded absently and said: "Barton Charles is one of the richest men in America. And the outlaw is right. Isobel is Bart's only child. He'll pay any amount of money for her safe return." His eyes lifted to Matt. "I have six men outside, all of them excellent soldiers. Is there any way of rushing the mayor's home and freeing my wife?"

Matt shook his head. "The result wound be a heap of dead troopers and maybe a dead wife. I don't advise it."

"Then what can we do?"

"Wait. Let Henry make a mistake and then hit him hard."

"Suppose he doesn't make a mistake?"

"Then we'll have to find another way."

Greenwood bowed his head, deep in thought. "Maybe I can talk to him. He might listen to reason if I tell him he can surrender to the Army."

"This is not an Army matter," Matt pointed out mildly. "It comes under my jurisdiction."

"I beg to differ, Marshal," the officer said. "Isobel is an Army wife, and that makes her abduction a military matter."

Matt shrugged. "Have it you own way, Lieutenant. But when the ball opens, I intend to deal with Henry and Waters in my own way."

Greenwood's eyes went to Matt's splinted leg. "Marshal, I hardly think you're in a condition to deal with anything. Let me handle it from now on. I can send a rider back to Fort Dodge for the rest of my troop, though that will take a couple of days because of the snow." The young officer slammed his fist into his open palm. "If I hit the outlaws with overwhelming force, they won't have time to do Isobel harm."

"And in the meantime?" Matt asked, suddenly irritated.

"In the meantime I'll talk to this man Henry and offer him surrender terms. Even the worst of outlaws may listen to reason."

Matt shook his head. "Lieutenant, Scar Henry is not a reasonable man and he's not about to surrender."

"Don't you think I should be the one to make that judgment, Marshal?"

"Suit yourself," Matt said. "But leave

your men behind. The sight of six cavalry troopers could make Scar real nervous and there's no telling what a nervous man will do." Matt stumped on his crutch to the rack and took down his coat and hat. "I'll come with you."

"That's really not necessary," Greenwood said.

"Humor me, Lieutenant," Matt said dryly. "It would make me feel so much better."

"Very well, then," the officer said, his exasperated expression revealing that he did not care for Matt's interference. "You and I will go alone. But first let me find quarters for my men and their mounts. They've ridden far and both the men and horses are tired."

"There's a livery stable down Front Street a ways where you can put up the horses," Matt said. "I'm sure quarters can be found for the troopers at the Dodge House."

"The barn will do nicely for both men and the horses, Marshal. Soldiers must not be mollycoddled."

"Learn that at the Point, did ye, Lieutenant?" Festus asked, his cool eyes judging the man.

"As a matter of fact I did," Greenwood said.

Festus nodded. "Figgered as much."

After Greenwood left to see to his men, Festus shook his head. "That's one pig-headed so'jer, Matthew. He'll end up getting' all of them boys with him killed."

"He's young yet, Festus, and he'll learn," Matt said. "Good judgment comes from experience, and a lot of that comes from bad judgment."

"You don't think ol' Scar will listen to him, do you?" the deputy asked.

"Not a chance," Matt answered.

When Greenwood returned, he and Matt left on foot for the mayor's house. The officer had left behind his holstered Colt and opened the top of his coat to show his soldier blue.

The young officer was obviously annoyed at Matt's slower pace and he showed it by scowling every time he had to wait for the big marshal to catch up. The snow was falling thickly and a keening wind drove off the plains. The morning was very cold, well below zero, and Matt's breath smoked as he struggled through the deepening drifts. There were few people on Front or Texas streets, though businessmen crowded Ma's Kitchen and the smell of coffee and frying bacon hung in the air.

Mayor Kelley's house seemed deserted

when Matt and Greenwood stopped outside the front porch, but the marshal saw a curtain twitch in the front parlor window and knew they were being watched.

"Mr. Henry!" Greenwood yelled.

There was no answer.

"Have they gone?" the officer asked Matt.

"They know we're here," the marshal answered. "Holler again."

"Mr. Henry!"

From inside a man's voice yelled: "What the hell do you want?" It was Henry.

"My name is Greenwood, first lieutenant, United States Army. I wish to talk to you."

"About your wife?"

"Yes. About my wife."

There was a long pause. Then the front door opened and Henry and Waters stepped onto the porch, Isobel between them.

Greenwood's face paled and the man suddenly looked upset. He glanced at Matt in confusion, his mouth working, and the big marshal said: "Scar, the lieutenant here wants to offer you terms."

Henry laughed. "The hell he does. What's your offer, soldier boy?"

Isobel stood very still, and her face registered absolutely no reaction to the sight of her husband.

The officer recovered his composure and said: "Mr. Henry, I want you to surrender your prisoners and then accompany me to Fort Dodge, where you will be tried by an Army court. I promise you a fair hearing and you will be represented by a capable lawyer."

"The hell you say," Henry yelled. "Well, here's my offer, soldier boy. You get in touch with your wife's daddy and tell him we're holding his daughter for ransom. If he ever wants to see her alive again, he'd better pay up right on time."

"Mr. Henry," Greenwood said, "I can have a whole troop of cavalry here in a couple of days. Surrender now or I'll take back my wife by force of arms."

"Is that so?" Henry said. "Well, listen good, Greenwood. If one Army boot steps on this porch, I'll scatter your wife's brains. I won't wait. I won't ask questions. I won't listen to reason. I'll just gun her. Get my drift?"

Desperately Greenwood tried another tack. "Mr. Henry, the telegraph wires are down. I won't be able to get in touch with Isobel's father, maybe for days."

"Don't you worry about that none,"

Henry said. "When we pull out of here, I'll tell you where Barton Charles can send the money. I'll be waiting."

"But, Mr. Henry —"

"You git, soldier boy, and you too, Dillon, or I'll quit jawing and start shooting."

Matt had his hand on the gun in his pocket, but he knew Henry did not want gunplay. Not now, when things were going so well for him. The guns would come later.

Greenwood turned and looked at Matt helplessly and the big marshal shrugged. "Don't waste any more breath, Lieutenant. I told you Henry was not a reasonable man."

The two men stood and watched Henry and Waters lead Isobel inside. Then they turned their steps back to the office.

"Sorry you wasted your time, Greenwood," Matt said.

The young officer smiled, surprising the marshal. "I thought I did rather well under the circumstances," he said.

"What makes you say that?" Matt asked, his surprise growing.

"Just that the woman on the porch was indeed very pretty — but she wasn't my wife."

Chapter 21

The Officer's Folly

When Matt and Greenwood returned to the office, Doc Adams was there, changing the dressing on Festus' shoulder. After the physician tied up the bandage, Matt introduced Greenwood and Doc shook his hand. "Sorry we meet under such trying circumstances," Doc said.

The officer nodded. "I'm confident I can handle the situation," he said, "though I may need to send for more men."

"You plan on storming the place?" Doc asked.

"In force," Greenwood replied.

"We already tried that," Doc said. "We didn't get Henry, and it cost us Kitty's saloon and the life of a good old man."

"Micah Lewis was all of that," Festus said, a small, heartfelt epitaph for the slain oldster.

"With all due respect, Doctor," Greenwood said, "there's a big difference between an untrained rabble of civilians and a troop of United States cavalry."

"Could be," Doc admitted, taking no offense. "But the result will be the same, more men dead on the ground and maybe your wife lying among them."

Doc had brought a platter of thick bacon sandwiches from the restaurant and Matt accepted one eagerly. He turned to Greenwood and asked: "If the woman with Henry and Waters wasn't your wife, then who was she?"

The officer shrugged. "I've no idea."

"What's all this about?" Doc asked.

"Henry thinks he's holding Isobel Charles-Greenwood prisoner. He isn't. Lieutenant Greenwood here says he's never seen the woman before in his life." Matt gave a small smile. "Since he's her husband, I reckon he should know."

Doc rubbed his chin, scowling, deep in thought. "Describe your wife, Greenwood," he said.

The young officer looked confused for a moment or two, then answered: "Well, she's this tall" — he placed his hand, palm down at the level of his shoulder — "and she's very slim with gray eyes and blondish hair."

"Is she small?" Doc asked. "And quite plain perhaps?"

Greenwood bristled. "I think she's beautiful," he snapped.

Doc was not put out in the least. "Yes, yes, I'm sure you do. But the description you just gave leads me to believe that your wife was traveling incognito — as a maid."

"A maid? Isobel? She'd never do that," Greenwood said. The man's face clouded in thought. "Unless . . ."

"Unless?" Doc prompted.

"Why, unless Isobel's father was afraid that traveling alone she might become a target for kidnappers. He could have paid another woman to take her place and had Isobel pose as her servant."

Matt stopped chewing and said: "If a kidnap attempt was made, they'd grab the decoy and not the real Isobel Charles-Greenwood. How much money would Barton Charles have to pay to hire a woman to set herself up as a target?"

"A great deal, I should imagine," Doc said. "He's a real fond papa, it seems. I'd say the decoy was glad to take the job because she figured Charles was just being an overprotective, paranoid parent and that a kidnapping was a very remote possibility."

"I wonder who the woman is," Festus said. "She sure acted uppity."

"Acted is correct, Festus," Kitty said. "She's an actress of some kind, I imagine. There are plenty of out-of-work actresses who'd jump at the chance to take Barton Charles' money and play the fine lady, if only for a few days."

"Then why has she kept her mouth shut until now?" Matt asked.

"Because she sees the chance of getting more money from a grateful Charles if she keeps up the facade," Kitty said. "But if it comes right down to it, and Henry starts to play rough, I think she'll point out the real Isobel quick enough."

"A common servant," Greenwood said, his face bleak, shaking his head. "My wife." The young officer stepped toward the door. "I have to see to my men."

"Lieutenant." A hard edge to Matt's voice stopped him in his tracks. "Don't do anything foolish. Sooner or later Henry will slip up and we can take him."

Without turning, Greenwood nodded, threw the door wide and walked outside.

Festus closed the door behind the officer. "I'd say that's one worried young man." He smiled.

"I don't blame him," Doc said. "If I was in his position, I'd be worried too."

"Henry has to make a move into the open soon," Matt said. "He can't stay holed up much longer."

Doc glanced out of the window. "He

might do just that, if this snow and cold continues."

Suddenly Doc's face became thoughtful again and he repeated quietly, more to himself than anyone else: "If this snow and cold continues." He rubbed his jaw. "Now that's a thought."

"What's on your mind, Doc?" Matt asked.

The physician shrugged. "Oh, it's nothing. Maybe nothing at all."

Later in the day, despite Matt's arguments, Kitty decided to take a room at the Dodge House.

"This office is starting to crowd in on me, Matt," she explained. "And besides, a woman needs her privacy."

"But what about Henry?" the marshal asked. "Kitty, I can't protect you at the hotel."

"I'll be all right, Matt," she answered. "Besides Mr. and Mrs. Kelley are there, and the mayor has his shotgun."

The marshal realized that Kitty's mind was made up and he'd learned a long time ago that there were many theories about winning an argument with a woman, but none of them work.

Matt insisted on walking Kitty to the

hotel, despite a warning from Doc that his leg was badly swollen and he needed rest. When he returned to the office the day was already shading into night and the lamps were being lit along Front Street. The snow had eased up some, but the temperature had dropped even further and Festus was concerned that they might soon run out of wood for the stove.

"If it comes right down to it, we'll burn the broken table first," he said. "Then your desk, Matthew."

"The weather has to break sometime," Matt said. "It can't go on like this much longer."

"I dunno about that," Festus said. "I mind one time when I were just a younker getting' caught in a line shack over to Montana way for the best part of four months one winter. Snowed every single day and got as cold as a mother-in-law's kiss at night."

"What did you do for all that time?"

"Well, there were some books there, the Bible an' a couple of others, but you know I'm not much of a hand for reading, so I whittled."

"Whittled?"

"Yup. Had a table in there big enough for four men to sit at, but by the spring thaw I had it down to the size of a nubbin no bigger'n my little finger. Whittled away the whole damn thing." Festus shook his head. "They took ten dollars out of my wages for the table, but it was worth it. Otherwise I'd have gone crazy bein' cooped up like that for so long."

"Well, let's hope this snow doesn't last four months," Matt said. "I'm not a whittling man."

"Me neither, Matthew," Festus said. "That table sure cured me o' whittlin' for life."

The two men talked on as the night deepened around the marshal's office, but at eight Matt rose, buckled on his gun belt and dressed in his coat and hat.

"I'm going to check on Kitty," he said. "It worries me some that she's not here."

"Want me to tag along, Matthew?" Festus asked.

Matt shook his head. "Best you stay here and keep an eye on things. Never can tell when —"

A sharp rattle of gunfire shattered the quiet of Dodge, followed by a brief silence, then the sound of more firing.

Matt grabbed his crutch and swung out of the door. Behind him Festus struggled into his mackinaw and grabbed the Greener.

"No, stay here, Festus," Matt told his deputy. "If I don't come back, get over to the Dodge House real quick and look out for Kitty."

The firing came from beyond the junction of Front and Texas streets — the direction of Mayor Kelley's house.

His crutch thumping on the ice-covered boardwalk, Matt hurried in the direction of the shooting. All was quiet now, but then he heard the thud of running booted feet coming toward him.

A cavalry trooper, his eyes wild, tried to run past, but Matt reached out and grabbed the man by the arm. "What happened?" he asked.

The soldier jerked his arm away. "They're all dead!" he yelled. "Johnson, Williams, Hargrove . . . all of them."

"Wait," Matt said as the trooper made to run again. "How did it hap—"

"Damn you, leave me be!" the soldier screamed, pushing the marshal away from him. "I've seen hell!"

Matt tried to grab the man, but the trooper eluded him and pounded at a run down the boardwalk in the direction of the livery stable, as though the devil himself was on his heels.

What lay ahead was partially obscured by the fine screen of the falling snow. Matt struggled along the boardwalk, then dragged through deep drifts where it ended. Ahead of him Mayor Kelley's house was in darkness, a sullen streak of gray gunsmoke hanging, just visible, across the open ground in front of the building.

Matt pulled his Colt and battled forward, the crutch slowing him. He was about thirty yards from the house when he saw a figure rise from the snow and stumble, bent over, toward him, the man's hand clutching his shoulder.

The big marshal stopped, his gun ready, as the man got closer. It was Lieutenant Greenwood and he was hit hard.

The young officer almost slammed into Matt, but the marshal sidestepped awkwardly at the last moment and put out his arm and steadied Greenwood.

"It was my fault," the soldier whispered, his face chalk white, eyes haunted. "It was all my fault."

"We're heading back to my office," Matt said. "Do you think you can make it?"

Greenwood nodded. Clumsy on his crutch, the big marshal supported the wounded officer as they pushed through the snow and regained the boardwalk.

Festus and another man Matt didn't recognize in the darkness helped them both the rest of the way.

Kitty, Doc Adams, Mayor Kelley and a few other men were crowded into the office when Matt and Greenwood were assisted inside. The lieutenant sank gratefully into Matt's chair; then Doc helped the soldier off with his coat and removed his tunic with its yellow officer's shoulder straps.

Doc examined the wound on Greenwood's shoulder and said: "The bullet's still in there. It's got to come out."

While Doc got his physician's bag, Kelley turned to Matt. "What happened? I heard all the shooting, and by the time I got here, I saw you headed back to the office."

Matt, his face expressionless, nodded to Greenwood. "Best ask him. He was there."

The young officer lifted haunted eyes to Kelley. "I thought we could rush the house under cover of the darkness. My men had almost reached the porch and I believed we had the battle just about won. Then that devil appeared."

"Who?" Kelley asked, his face paling as all his old-country superstitions bubbled to the surface. "In the name of God, man, what devil?"

Greenwood shook his head. “I don’t know who he is . . . a man with two guns. I never saw anyone shoot like that. He just stood there, laughing, his guns blazing that terrible orange flame. Five of my men went down in just a couple of seconds. Then I was hit. One . . . one of my troopers saved himself. He . . . he ran away.”

“I met him,” Matt said. “I reckon he’s still running.”

The young officer looked at Matt and touched his tongue to dry lips. “That man with the two guns, he wasn’t human. Only a demon from the lowest reaches of hell could shoot like that.”

“Oh, he’s human all right,” Matt said, trying to curb his anger over the young officer’s folly in attacking the house. For now at least, Greenwood had suffered enough. “His name is Deacon Waters and he’s fast, very fast with the revolver.” The big marshal hesitated, then added: “He’s maybe the fastest there ever was.”

Chapter 22

A Student of History

After Doc Adams removed the bullet from Greenwood's shoulder and bandaged the wound, a gloomy silence lay heavy in the marshal's office, as though everyone present were confronting thoughts they feared to deal with.

Finally Mayor Kelley's eyes slid from the window and he said to no one in particular, looking into dead space in front of him: "The snow has stopped."

Matt stepped to the window and glanced outside. Only a few stray flurries tossed in the wind and the sky above Dodge was clearing. A handful of stars had appeared but the night was very cold. A hard frost had settled on the town, lacing windows with a labyrinth of flowers, gleaming like sheet steel on the warped timbers of the shadowed buildings. Icicles hung from every ledge, eave and corner and trapped the orange glows from the scattered streetlamps like fireflies in amber.

"Come morning, I'll give Henry the

money from the town banks and maybe he'll leave," Kelley said, talking to Matt's wide back. Unspoken by the mayor, but nevertheless hanging very loud in the room, was the outlaw's demand that Kitty go with him. "There's no other way out of this terrible mess."

Matt turned. He saw Kelley's strained, pale face. The faces of the other three townsmen in the room were expressionless, like they'd been carved out of marble. Kitty stood close to Greenwood, who sat with his head lowered, his mouth slack, a man unable to fully grasp the magnitude of the disaster that had befallen his small command.

Out there, lying in the snow, very still, very quiet, were the bodies of five Buffalo Soldiers, killed by a man who knew the way of the six-shot revolver better than anyone else then alive.

A fierce anger burned in Matt Dillon, not directed at Greenwood, but at himself. He felt powerless, helpless, like a man who has lost his way. He wanted to lash out at Henry and Waters, beat and smash both of them to a pulp with his bare fists. But, his frustration growing, he knew that if the mayor had his way he would have to stand idly by and watch them ride out of town.

Matt thrust the thought from his head. That was not going to happen. No matter what, he would not let Henry and Waters leave Dodge City alive. He would be their judge, jury and executioner, and as they had done to the soldiers, he vowed to visit Hell on them.

Kelley spoke up again, interrupting Matt's train of thought. "Well, we all might as well turn in. We're sure not doing any good standing around here with long faces." He turned to Kitty. "Miss Kitty, may I escort you back to the hotel?"

Before the woman could answer, Doc said: "Hold up there, Kelley. I have an idea."

"Let's hear it, Doc," the mayor said. "About now we're running mighty short on ideas and I'll consider anything."

The physician turned to Greenwood. "Lieutenant," he said, "are you a student of history?"

The soldier lifted dull, hurting eyes to Doc. "Maybe. I guess so. I was taught military history at the Point."

"Did they tell you what the Russians did when Napoléon invaded their country in 1812?"

Greenwood, weakened by loss of blood and the pain in his shoulder, made a visible effort to collect his thoughts. Finally he asked: "The battles? Or do you mean scorched earth?"

"Exactly. Scorched earth. The Russians burned everything in the French army's path, leaving the soldiers no food, their horses no fodder. Napoléon discovered every village burned and deserted, the people gone. In the end, his Grand Army found only starvation and death."

"Doc," Kelley said uneasily, his wary eyes holding on the physician, "what's all that got to do with Dodge City?"

"Everything," Doc answered. "You said earlier you'd meet Henry's demands tomorrow morning. But suppose you're not here? Suppose there's no one in Dodge he can talk to? What good will his demands do him then? He won't be able to kill anymore, because we'll all be gone."

Warming to his plan, Doc added: "We remove every scrap of food from town and take it with us. We take the money from the banks and then we leave. All of us, every single living soul in Dodge, even the dogs. When Henry wakes up tomorrow morning he'll find a ghost town."

"But . . . but that's a lot of people," Kelley said. "I know most folks leave town in winter, but we're still talking a couple of hundred souls, including the old and the sick. Where would we go?"

"To the snowbound train," Doc said triumphantly. "We load the aged and the infirm into wagons, bundle them up real good and carry our firewood with us. We can light the stoves in the carriages and we'll have enough food to last us for days."

Doubt clouded Kelley's face and he turned to Matt. "Marshal, can it be done? And what will become of Mrs. Charles-Greenwood?"

Hope flared in Matt. This could be his chance to finally get Henry and Waters out in the open. He nodded to one of the townsmen standing around Kelley. "Monahan, go get McIntyre, that train engineer. He and his fireman have been sleeping at the depot. If anyone knows if the train can accommodate two hundred people, it's him."

Monahan nodded and left. Then Greenwood looked at Matt and asked: "You never answered the question, Marshal. What about my wife?"

"The town won't be completely deserted," Matt said. "Festus and me will stay behind, hidden someplace. When Henry and Waters make their move to leave, we'll be waiting."

The young lieutenant stiffened in shock. "But you're no match for Waters. Even if you weren't crippled, you couldn't stop him. Remember, I saw the man shoot and he's deadly with guns."

Matt nodded. "He is all that. But I'm pretty good with a gun my ownself."

"And he's got me," Festus said. "And, Mr. Lieutenant Greenwood, I ain't no bargain."

The young officer's eyes slanted in horror from Matt to Festus and back again. Then he let his chin slump on his chest. "I'll never see my wife again," he whispered. "It's over."

When McIntyre, the engineer, arrived, Matt told him Doc's plan and then asked if the abandoned train could take a couple of hundred people. "At a pinch," the man answered. "We could put the younger, fitter men in the boxcar and start a fire in there." The man's brow knotted in thought for a while; then he nodded. "Yup, I reckon it could be done. We'll be crowded though, and no mistake."

"Mayor Kelley, start spreading the word," Doc said. "Tell everyone to assemble at the end of town farthest away from your home — behind the Dodge House is a good place — and tell them to keep it quiet. Not a sound. Tell them to muzzle their dogs if they have to."

"And listen," Matt added, "I want every horse in town gone. Take Buck and Ruth and the mounts of the dead soldiers. The outlaws have their horses at the livery stable. Take those too. I want Henry and Waters to have no way out of Dodge.

"When you've done that, send a man on a fast horse to the fort for help. If things don't work out the way I plan, maybe even Henry and Waters will realize it's hopeless to battle a full troop of cavalry."

"That's all well and good, but suppose the people don't want to leave?" Kelley asked, the skin of his face tightening in desperation.

"Mayor," Doc said patiently, "everybody in town has money in the banks. If you tell them they have a choice of leaving or having the outlaw Scar Henry ride out with their hard-earned savings, I believe they'll gladly opt to leave. And if they refuse," Doc added, his face suddenly harsh and uncompromising, "you'll just have to make them. There's been enough killing in Dodge and we don't want more."

"Well, I'll try," Kelley said.

"Don't try, Mayor," Doc snapped, irritated beyond measure. "Damn it, man! Just do it, is all."

After Kelley and the other townsmen left to spread the word, Matt stepped beside Doc and asked: "Do you really think they'll leave?"

The physician shook his head. "Matt, I don't know, but I sure hope so. Maybe a few will be prepared to stand by and watch Henry ride out with their money, but most will realize that if all the banks are robbed the town will be ruined — and them with it."

"I hope you're right, Doc," Matt said.

Doc's smile was slight. "So do I."

Kitty had been silent for a long time. Now, her face clouded by worry, she asked: "Matt, if we all leave, where will you and Festus go? You can't stay here. It will be the first place Henry will look."

The big marshal nodded. "I've thought about that. I reckon we'll hole up in a place Henry won't suspect — the Long Branch. We can hunker down in the ruins and watch the street."

Kitty bit her lip. "Matt, Lieutenant Greenwood is right. You're no match for a gunman like Deacon Waters."

"Now don't you go doubting me as well, Kitty." Matt smiled. "I've met two-gun tinhorns before, and I'm still here."

"You're crazy," Greenwood said bitterly.

"This whole idea of abandoning the town is crazy. Why not just wait until help arrives from the fort?"

"Because by then Henry and Waters would be long gone and your wife with them, to say nothing of the town's money," Matt answered. "And there's another thing. Every moment that passes puts your wife's life in more danger. It's only a matter of time before Henry gets told which woman is the real Mrs. Charles-Greenwood and he could kill her out of spite. You're a rational man, Lieutenant, but you're dealing here with the irrational. Scar Henry is far from sane and there's no telling what he'll do."

Greenwood opened his mouth to say something, but then his face took on a defeated, hopeless look and he lapsed into silence.

Matt stepped to the window and looked outside. Kelley must have ordered all the lamps along Front Street to be extinguished because everything was dark except for the pale sheen of the snow and the frost. More stars were appearing and even the wind had dropped, as though tired from its exertions of the past few days.

The marshal felt anxiety rise in him. The whole plan depended on the utmost secrecy. If Henry and Waters realized what was happening, they would move to stop it, and that would result in more dead men in the street.

He could only hope that the two outlaws, flushed by their victory over the soldiers, would have lowered their vigilance, fearing no more attacks that night.

But Scar Henry was a cautious man, and that was a mighty uncertain thing.

Outside, the street was quiet, deserted, wrapped in darkness.

Then the people of Dodge started to come. . . .

Chapter 23

Exodus

They came singly and in families, moving like gray ghosts through the night.

People came from the white-painted mansions across the tracks, and from the mean shacks and shanties behind the saloons along Front and Texas streets.

Some wore furs. Others were wrapped in ragged blankets. All trudged slowly and silently through the snow, moving toward the assembly point behind the Dodge House.

"Doc," Matt exclaimed, "your plan worked! They're leaving."

The physician hurried beside Matt and watched as the townspeople shuffled past, heads bent, faces strained, looking like a beaten army.

But they were leaving . . . all of them.

Matt quickly donned his coat and hat, grabbed his crutch and stepped outside, Kitty, Festus and Doc at his heels. He joined the silent march, nodding to a man here, touching his hat to a woman there.

Somewhere along the column a child cried, and its mother hushed it.

The town bankers had already opened their premises, and in complete darkness, moneybags were being passed from hand to hand and loaded into a freight wagon. Another wagon held firewood and food gathered from the shelves of the general stores, and the door of Ma's Kitchen stood wide-open, as men carried out sacks of flour and slabs of bacon.

Behind the Dodge House, Mayor Kelley had assembled three more wagons, and Matt marveled at the man's organizational ability on such short notice. The old and the infirm were bundled into blankets and helped or carried into the wagon beds, all with very few words uttered and little complaint.

It seemed that the people of Dodge knew well what was at stake for their town and were determined to save it, no matter the personal cost in cold and discomfort.

And it was cold . . . very cold.

Everyone's breath smoked in the frigid air, rising above the assembled people in a gray cloud, and the flanks of the draft horses, shaggy with their winter coats, were frosted white.

More people arrived in the crowding

darkness and stood around, stamping their feet, blowing on blue-veined hands, waiting.

Big Jed Owens, the banker, bundled into a fur coat, stepped beside Matt, his face bleak, the eyes he turned to the marshal dull with regret. "Jane Morgan wouldn't come, Marshal," he said. "I tried to convince her but she's in a world of her own now, sitting in the dark, staring at the wall. My wife brought along her children, but Jane refused to leave. I don't think she listened to me or she didn't know what I was saying. She will soon die of grief, that poor woman."

Matt nodded, remembering. "Thanks, Jed. You did all you could."

"It wasn't enough," the banker said. "I fell way short."

Owens suddenly looked old and tired. He turned away from Matt and helped his wife get Jane Morgan's youngsters into a wagon. The marshal felt a spike of unease. It was unlikely the woman would be discovered, but right now it was just a small complication he didn't need.

Kitty's face was lost in the shadow of her cloak hood when she walked to the marshal's side. "They came, Matt," she said. "Every single one of them."

"They know what's at stake, for themselves and this town," Matt said. "They made the right choice."

"And you?" Kitty asked, raising her face to the marshal. Her hood slipped back on her head and Matt read the concern in her eyes.

"Yes, I'm making the right choice, Kitty," he answered. "Men like Henry and Waters have to be stopped. Evil might triumph for a while, but in the end it can be defeated by our own endurance and will. I can't let them ride out of Dodge and spread their evil in some other town."

"Nothing I can say will change you mind, will it?"

Matt shook his head. "No. It's time for me to make a stand, Kitty. I won't allow Henry and Waters to brag that they got away with murder and robbery in Matt Dillon's town."

Kitty seemed to realize that further argument was useless. "Then you take care, Matt Dillon. I want you here waiting for me when I get back."

"I'll be here," he said. "You can count on it."

"Sorry to interrupt," Kelley said, stepping beside Matt. "But we're about ready to leave."

"Everybody here?" Matt asked. He glanced over at the small horse herd. "And all the horses in town?"

"Near as I can tell." Kelley hesitated. "I suppose Owens told you about Mrs. Morgan."

The marshal nodded. "He told me."

Kelley shook his head. "Sad, very sad."

"Better get going, Mayor," Matt said.

"The shallows of the Arkansas to the west of town are frozen solid," Kelley said. "We'll cross there. I don't want to take the wagons and all these people over the bridge. Too much noise." The mayor smiled. "You know, I feel like Moses leading the Israelites to the Promised Land."

"You don't need to go all the way to the Promised Land, Mayor," Matt said. "Just get to the train."

"We should make it by sunup if the weather holds." Kelley glanced at the sky. "Looks good. Not a cloud in sight."

Matt lifted Kitty onto the tailgate of a wagon and held her hand until the driver slapped the team into motion. "Be waiting for me, Matt," she said.

The marshal nodded, but he didn't know if Kitty saw him as he watched her wagon become one with the darkness.

A couple of men brought Lieutenant

Greenwood from the marshal's office and helped him into one of the other wagons. The soldier settled himself, then stuck out his hand. "We've had our differences, Marshal," he said. "But good luck to you."

Matt shook the officer's hand and watched until he too disappeared into the gloom.

Then it was Kelley's turn. "Matt," he said, "are you sure you don't want me to leave a couple of men behind? Newly O'Brien maybe?"

Matt shook his head. "Mayor, you pay Festus and me to be the law in Dodge. Now we got it to do."

Kelley nodded, accepting the way of things. "Then good luck, Matt. And see you shoot straight."

"I aim to," the marshal said, not a trace of humor on his face.

The mayor lingered for a few moments, like a man who wanted to express his tangled thoughts but couldn't find the words. Finally he said: "Matt, it's been a long time for you and me. A lot of years through good times and bad. Since I've known you, you've always stood tall and I never once saw you take a backward step from any man."

Matt knew Kelley had just composed his

epitaph and he accepted it for what it was, the man's well-meaning attempt to express his respect. The mayor obviously did not expect his marshal to last through the following day.

Kelley had said what he needed to say and now Matt was willing to let it go. "Better get on your way, Mayor. Moses should be at the front of the column."

The little Irishman nodded, his Celtic sentimentality misting his eyes. Then, as though ashamed of himself for showing such emotion, he lifted his hand in farewell and hurried to join the others.

Matt and Festus stood and watched the last wagon leave, people walking beside its slow churning wheels. And when it was gone, Dodge was lost to silence and the deepening night, the snow sleeping cold under the vast sky.

Chapter 24

Night Music of the Henry

Matt and Festus returned to the marshal's office and gathered up their long guns, including the Henry. Matt stuck a couple of cups in his pocket, a small package of tea and the extra boxes of shells.

After Festus turned off the oil lamp, the two lawmen crossed Front Street to the ruined Long Branch.

A pale moon spread a halo of silver light across the sky, and now that the whole town was in darkness, the stars were so bright and close, a man might think he could reach out and grab a handful and let them trickle, frosty and shining, through his fingers.

The coyotes, never ones to miss an opportunity, were scavenging all over town knowing that the human and canine threats were gone. On cat feet, shadowy shapes shifted shamelessly through the hushed gloom, coming and going, exploring the alleys, snuffling around on the boardwalks in front of the empty, echoing buildings.

From somewhere close by, Matt heard an owl question the night, only to be mocked by the scornful hiss of the rising wind.

The force of the explosion had blown out all the windows of the Long Branch, and Matt and Festus crunched though shards of shattered glass as they took up a position behind the front wall of the building. From there they could look out on the street without being seen, at least as long as the night lasted. Matt found an upturned chair and brought it closer to the wall. He sat and propped his crutch against his leg, the Henry across his thighs.

"Matthew, what you reckon will happen when ol' Scar wakes up an' finds hisself in a ghost town?" Festus asked, his face lost in the darkness.

"I don't know," Matt answered. "But whatever he does, I plan on being ready for him."

Festus was silent for a long while, then said: "Matthew, what do you reckon our chances are of gettin' out o' this alive?"

It was a good question and Matt could not immediately find an answer. After giving it some thought, he said, a smile in his voice, "Festus, if I was a betting man, I'd put my money on Henry and Waters because I'd reckon our chances were mighty slim."

"Then why are we doing it, Matthew?"

"Because we're here. There's nobody else but us." Matt hesitated, then added: "And you and me, Festus, we wear the tin stars."

"Ever think to be anything else but a lawman?" the deputy asked.

"No, I never do. Maybe one day I'll think about getting me a little spread someplace. But right now, tonight, I don't want to be anything else but a lawman. I've got too many scores to settle."

"Me neither," Festus said, "about not being a lawman, I mean. But I'd sure give my right arm to have a dozen Texas Rangers with us, settin' close by an' ready."

"Me too, Festus," Matt said, talking into the darkness. "And maybe a regiment of cavalry."

The marshal heard Festus shift his feet, a shiver in his voice. "Getting colder," he said. "It's gonna be a long night."

"It's going to warm up soon," Matt said. "See, I don't plan on letting Henry and Waters get any sleep. I want them good and tired come sunup. A tired man makes mistakes."

"What's your plan, Matthew?"

Festus stepped closer and Matt could see the white gleam of his face. "Let's make a small fire where it can't be seen from the street and brew up that tea I brought. Then I'll tell you."

"Geez, Matthew, that's gonna make ol' Scar mad enough to kick a hog barefoot," Festus said. "Think we can do it without bein' seen?"

Matt tried his tea and found it good and hot. "The town is so dark, we can stay out of sight until first light. I've been doing some calculating and I figure between us we can keep Henry and Waters awake all night. That ought to slow them down some when they appear come morning."

Matt turned his head slightly, looking at his deputy. "Remember, one shot every fifteen minutes and keep them high, Festus. We don't want to hit the women in the house. Shoot. Then fog it out of there and find yourself another position. Wait fifteen minutes and shoot again." Matt shifted in his rickety chair, the slender legs creaking under his weight. "We'll do two-hour shifts, and as soon as I finish this tea, I'll start the ball rolling."

"What time is it, Matthew?" Festus asked.

Matt reached into his coat, took his watch from his vest pocket and tilted the timepiece so the face caught a sliver of light from outside. "Almost midnight. Time I was going."

Matt rose, picked up the Henry and asked his deputy: "Think you can shoot well enough off your left shoulder?"

"Well enough to hit a house, Matthew. I don't reckon that calls for much in the way o' marksmanship."

"Keep your eyes skinned, then," Matt said. He tucked his crutch under his arm. "See you in a couple of hours."

"Step careful, Matthew," Festus said. "It may be dark out there, but the night has eyes."

The big marshal left the saloon and stepped out into the quiet of the moonlight. He crossed the street and reached the opposite boardwalk, then, his crutch thumping, made his awkward way toward Mayor Kelley's house.

Matt crossed the junction with Texas Street, and when the boardwalk ended at the last of the commercial buildings, he stepped off and faded into the shadows.

Kelley's house was now in sight, a few lights showing, reflecting faintly on the bodies of the dead troopers lying still in the snow. Matt followed the wall of the last building, and when he reached the corner, he stopped. Behind him, he saw only darkness and the vague bulk of a few scattered shacks and a small pole corral. Nearby a cottonwood spread thin, white arms over a narrow creek coming off the Arkansas.

The moon was almost full, but to Matt's relief, it shed little light. He would shoot from here, then make his way to the cover of the shacks, where he would not be seen from the house.

Matt levered a round into the brass chamber of the Henry, the metallic *click-clack* loud in the silence. He sighted carefully on a lighted window of the house, raised his aim to one of the top panes and fired.

Glass shattered, immediately followed by a man's angry curse. The big marshal grinned and turned, pushing through the snow toward the dark cover of the shacks.

Behind him, he heard a door slam open and Henry yell: "Who the hell is out there? I'll kill you for this!"

Matt reached the nearest shack and ducked behind it, clumsy and slow on his crutch. He waited for a few seconds, then looked around the corner to the Kelley house.

Henry was out on the porch with a rifle, still cursing. The outlaw fired into the darkness, a couple of wild, angry shots that went nowhere.

"Dillon, damn you, is that you out there?" Henry yelled. The echoing silence mocked him, and the outlaw yelled again: "I swear to God I'm going to gun you, Dillon. I'm going to blow your guts out for sure." Grumbling, Henry stomped back inside and the night fell silent again.

Matt moved. He made his way back to the boardwalk and took up a position at the corner of the last building. A few yards away was the false-fronted Lone Star Saloon, its doorway recessed several feet. In fifteen minutes he would shoot and then make his way back there.

The lamps were suddenly dowsed at the Kelley home, plunging the building into darkness and Matt smiled. Good — he had them rattled.

Slow minutes ticked past, Matt's breath smoking in the frigid air. The moon was dropping lower in the sky, its scant light thinning even more. But Matt's eyes were becoming accustomed to the dark and he could see well enough, except where the shadows angled deep at the corners of Kelley's house.

The wind now and then lifted fragile laces of snow from the tops of the drifts and whispered around Matt's ears, icy cold, indifferent to his comfort.

Matt took his watch from his pocket. Only twelve minutes had passed, but, tired of this inactivity, the marshal decided that twelve was close enough.

The windows of the Kelley house were all in darkness, but all he had to do was hit the building. The Henry's big .44.40 slug would smash through the thin timbers of the home and keep those inside on edge.

"All right, Scar, here's a little more Henry for Henry," Matt whispered aloud. And he triggered another shot.

The reaction from inside was almost immediate.

As though they'd been waiting for another bullet, Henry and Waters ran onto the porch, their guns blazing. But they were again firing at phantoms, spraying useless bullets into the darkness.

Praying that Festus would not be confused and come running, Matt raised the rifle to his shoulder and fired three fast shots at the men on the porch and saw them scamper inside. He wasn't sure in the darkness, but he thought he saw Henry flinch. Maybe he'd winged him.

But now Waters had reappeared and was firing at where he'd seen the flare of Matt's rifle. A bullet chewed wood just inches above the marshal's head and another kicked up an angry V of ice at his feet. It was time to move.

Matt had thought to retreat to the shelter of the saloon doorway, but he changed his mind and headed back along the boardwalk as quickly as his crutch would allow. Then, after twenty yards or so, he crossed to the other side of Front Street.

He ducked into a dark alley and leaned his back against the wall of one of the buildings, breathing hard, the emphatic beat of his hammering heart loud in his ears.

Waters was no longer shooting, but he heard Henry curse, the man so angry he was almost raving. In the silence of Dodge, the outlaw's voice traveled far, and Matt turned his head to listen.

"Kelley, you damned Irishman, are you out there?" Henry yelled.

There was a few minutes' pause as the outlaw waited for an answer. Then he called out again, his voice cracking with rage. "Kelley, call off your dogs. If another bullet hits this house, I'll kill these women and then every damn rube in Dodge, starting with you." The man waited, then yelled: "Do you hear me, Kelley?"

Matt heard the angry slam of a door, then silence. The marshal grinned. Henry was starting to get shook and he possibly had lead in him. Things were looking up!

But did the man mean what he said about killing the two women? Matt doubted it. The woman he thought was Mrs. Charles-Greenwood meant a lot of money to him and he was not about to lose his meal ticket. But suppose he decided to shoot the maid — the real heiress?

If the impostor had not yet revealed the truth, Henry would know that Mayor Kelley and the rest of the Dodge citizens would scarcely care about what he did to a lowly maid from back east.

Matt made up his mind. He couldn't back off now. There was too much at stake and he'd just have to assume that Henry was bluffing. The marshal knew he was playing with the lives of the two young women, but right now there was no other way.

Like everyone else in Dodge, including Festus and him, they would just have to take their chances.

It was a hard thought, but Matt Dillon

lived by a hard code and within that code there was little room for compromise or sentiment.

He would do what he had to do.

Fifteen minutes later, smiling, he smashed another bullet into the Kelley house.

"Just keep it going, Festus," Matt told his deputy after he returned to the dubious shelter of the Long Branch. "I think I winged Henry, and right now those two killers are getting mighty testy."

Festus handed Matt a steaming cup. "I brewed up some more tea," he said. "Figured you'd need it."

The marshal nodded his thanks as his deputy took up his rife. "Be careful, Festus," Matt said. "Just shoot and slide."

"Afore I go, one thing's been botherin' me, Matthew," Festus said, his face pinched and pale in the gloom. "Come mornin' when we meet up with Waters . . . how we gonna handle him? He's real gun slick that one."

Matt's smile was tight, his voice hard-edged and grim. "I'll handle him, Festus. If need be, I'll fight him right at the muzzle. That way, even when I'm going down, I won't miss."

Festus nodded, one fighting man's appreciation for another writ plain on his face. "I jes' wondered, Matthew, was all." Now his growing concern was out in the open, the deputy seemed relieved. "Like I said, I jes' wondered."

Festus left a few minutes later and a short while after that Matt heard the flat statement of his first rifle shot.

As he closed his eyes and tried to doze off in his chair, Matt had no worries about his deputy. During his years with the Rangers, Festus had fought both Comanche and Apache and he knew how to use cover and move in the darkness. Unshaven, shabby and illiterate, Festus Haggen was an easy man to underestimate — as several hard cases, all rattles and horns, had learned to their cost.

Even crippled, firing off his left shoulder, he was a dangerous man . . . and not one to be taken lightly.

Just after four, Festus shook Matt awake. "Ol' Deke Waters came after me, so plum riled he was spittin' spite," the deputy said. "I didn't trust my shooting, so I just fogged it out o' there an' lost him in the dark."

Matt thought it through. So Waters and Henry were prepared to leave the house to track down the riflemen who were making their lives miserable. Matt would have to be careful. He couldn't walk as fast as Festus.

Chapter 25

A Fugitive

Matt crossed the railroad tracks, then took up a position where he could see the rear of the Kelley house. He was on the lace-curtain side of town, a collection of large, sprawling homes most with carriage barns and pole corrals behind them.

He would be shooting at a distance of a quarter mile, and in the dark, but the mayor's home was a big target. More to the point, even slowed as he was by his crutch, he could easily fade back into the shadowed cover of the surrounding houses if Henry and Waters came looking for him.

The nearest home, a two-story affair with a couple of barns out back, lay just twenty yards behind him. He would have plenty of time to shoot, then get back into the deep shadows around the house, and the outlaws would have to cross a long stretch of open ground if they came after him.

Matt raised the Henry to his shoulder, held his breath and sighted on the dark bulk of the Kelley house. He fired, fired again, then shifted position.

The door of the mayor's house crashed open, and Matt heard booted feet pound onto the porch. But this time Henry and Waters did not fire blindly into the night. Matt couldn't see from this distance, but he figured the outlaws were looking around, their eyes trying to penetrate the surrounding darkness.

Henry yelled something Matt could not make out, then lapsed into silence.

A few minutes ticked past. Then Waters appeared, moving out of the gloom across the snow, heading right toward Matt's position. Henry, a rifle in his hands, walked a few yards behind him.

Matt blasted a shot at Waters, saw the man drop, then quickly hobbled a few yards to his right. Had he hit the gunman?

That question was answered a split second later when Waters rose on one knee and hammered four fast rounds at the spot where Matt had been standing. The gunman fired again and the big lawman heard his bullets rip the fabric of the night as he dusted to the left and right of his previous mark. One of Waters' bullets shattered the stock of the Henry, wrenching the rifle from Matt's hand. The gun spun away from him, dropping into the snow several feet from where he stood.

Behind Waters, Scar Henry fired. His shot was wide but close enough that Matt swore it had raised a blister on his hide.

The marshal knew he dared not pull his Colt and fire again. He couldn't match Waters' shooting skill, and for him the distance and the darkness ruled out accurate revolver work. If he fired a shot, the outlaws would nail him like a butterfly to a board.

Moving as quietly as he could, Matt eased back, angling to his right, trying to fade back into the gloom. A bullet probed for him, then another, but the outlaws had lost him.

"Deke, where the hell is he?" Henry yelled. "Was it Dillon?"

"It was Dillon all right," Waters answered. "And he's still out there someplace."

"The hell with him," Henry said. "We'll get him come first light. I don't like leaving those women back at the house by themselves."

Matt reached the corner of the two-story home and stood in the deep shadow cast by the high timber wall. His chest rising and falling, he held his Colt up and ready, hammer back, determined to cut loose if Henry and Waters got closer. But the two outlaws stayed back, not wanting to walk blindly into another man's gun.

"Matt Dillon, can you hear me?" It was Waters' voice.

The marshal made no answer. The gunman might be trying to locate his position.

He heard Waters laugh. "I know you're out there, and I know you can hear me, so listen up good," he yelled. "At first light, I'm going to come looking for you, and I'm going to end it." There was a few moments' pause. Then Waters hollered again. "No hard feelings, Matt. It's just something I have to do."

Matt waited until he heard the door of Kelley's house slam shut. Then he made his way back across the tracks, staying to the shadows.

The shooting was all done for tonight. He had accomplished his goal of keeping Henry and Waters awake. There would be little sleep for the outlaws since they would fear another attack on the house and would be on edge and alert.

As to how much a lack of sleep might slow them come morning, Matt had no idea. The big marshal smiled grimly to himself. Again he knew he was clutching at straws, and this one too might be grabbed away from him. Certainly Henry and Waters had looked plenty awake enough, and full of fight. When the ball opened at first light, sleepy or no, they'd be on the prod and looking for him. In effect, nothing had changed, Matt decided. Come the gray dawn he would still have a rendezvous with death.

The marshal crossed Front Street and stomped along the boardwalk toward the Long Branch. He was halfway there when he heard Henry yell something from the porch of the Kelley house. Then a shot hammered apart the silence of the night.

Matt stopped in his tracks. Was Henry shooting at him? That was unlikely. Then at who?

Drawing his Colt, Matt halted where he was, his eyes scanning the darkness around him. All was quiet, the buildings on either side of the street lost in motionless shadow. The coyotes, perhaps frightened by the roar of guns, had left town, though he could still hear them calling to one another out on the prairie. And everywhere lay the deep, fallen snow and the slick ice, the dreadful cold a living thing, born to nip and pinch and torment.

Matt saw something in an alley opposite, a narrow tunnel of blackness between a hardware store to his left and Ma's Kitchen. It had been just a brief flicker of white that was there for a moment and then gone.

Where were Henry and Waters? Could it have been one of them?

The big lawman glanced warily around him and saw nothing. Ungainly on his crutch, he stepped clumsily and heavily off the boardwalk, a sudden pain shooting through his broken leg. He walked into the middle of the street, then angled to his left, shielded from anyone in the alley by the bulk of the hardware store.

He reached the opposite boardwalk and, gun ready at waist level, hobbled carefully to the entrance of the alley. Matt stuck his head around the corner and said quietly: "You in there, come out now with your hands in the air."

His only answer was the clink of a bottle as someone's careless foot moved in the darkness.

"Right," Matt said, louder this time, his voice hard. "If you don't come out, I'm gonna cut loose, and I'll drill you square."

"No. Please don't shoot." A woman's voice.

"Then come on out — now," the marshal demanded.

A few moments passed. Then a small girl wearing only a white shift, her feet bare, stepped out of the alley and stood in the snow at the end of the boardwalk, shivering as she looked up fearfully at Matt.

The marshal blinked, unable to quite believe what he was seeing. It was the little maid or, in reality, Mrs. Isobel What's-her-name.

"What are you doing here?" Matt asked, realizing how ridiculous his question was as soon as he uttered it.

"I escaped," Isobel said. "When all the shooting started and Henry and the other man left the house, I crawled through the kitchen window."

Matt smiled. "I know someone else who did that." Now he noticed that the girl was shivering, her teeth chattering, the thin cotton of the shift doing nothing to keep out the searching cold. The big marshal reached down his hand, and after a moment's hesitation, the girl took it and he pulled her up onto the boardwalk. Matt quickly shrugged out of his sheepskin coat and placed it around Isobel's shoulders.

"I've got to get you back to the Long

Branch before you catch your death," he said.

The girl looked fearfully over her shoulder. "I think Henry will be coming after me," she said.

Matt hesitated. "Does he know who you really are?"

The girl shook her head. "Not yet. At least I don't think so."

"Then he won't be coming after you, not tonight. Scar Henry believes he has what he wants, and until he's told otherwise, you don't matter much to him."

"I do matter a great deal to my husband," Isobel said. "I saw all those soldiers killed. Then John fell. Is he . . . is he . . . ?"

"He's wounded, but he'll be fine," Matt said.

He briefly told her about the exodus of the people from Dodge, then said: "Your lieutenant is with them. You'll see him soon."

Matt led the trembling girl, lost inside his coat, across the street and along the boardwalk to the Long Branch.

An unspoken question on Festus' haggard, hairy face greeted them when they walked inside, and the marshal explained. "Mrs. What's-her-name escaped."

"Charles-Greenwood," Isobel supplied,

and despite everything that had happened to her, she managed to sound annoyed.

The deputy grinned and nodded. "Right glad to make your acquaintance, ma'am. I'm Deputy Marshal Festus Haggen an' I'm at your service."

Isobel smiled. "Thank you, Deputy Haggen. You're very kind."

After looking around the ruined saloon, Matt found a comfortable leather chair and pushed it toward the front wall. "Might as well sit," he told the girl. "It's still a ways until sunup."

The girl nodded gratefully and curled up in the chair, wrapping the marshal's coat around her.

"Would you care for tea, ma'am?" Festus asked, as though he was playing host in the polished parlor of a home across the tracks and not in the ruin of a cowtown saloon.

"I'd love a cup," Isobel said. "I'm so cold."

When the deputy left to brew the tea, Matt pushed his chair close to the girl and sat. "How come that other gal didn't tell Henry who you really are?" he asked. "Seems to me, it would be the logical thing for her to do."

Isobel smiled. "Unfortunately, Marshal, Anne Purdy is not logical. She's an out-of-work actress my father hired to pretend to be me since he feared a kidnap attempt on my journey from Saint Louis. He paid her a thousand dollars."

"Careful man," Matt smiled. "And a big spender."

The girl shrugged. "Father reads the newspapers and he thinks the West is a wild and dangerous place."

"Right now I'm inclined to agree with him," the marshal said. He shifted his weight in his chair. "So why hasn't Anne Purdy turned you in yet?"

"The oldest reason of all — she's in love. With Henry."

"In love with Scar Henry!" Matt was stunned. "How can that be?"

Isobel shrugged. "Who knows why a woman falls in love. Anne told me she'd read all the dime novels, and she's fascinated by the danger and mystery surrounding outlaws. When she first set eyes on Henry with that terrible scar and then saw how he could take over an entire town, she fell for him hard. Strange as it may seem, he's her kind of man."

Matt shook his head. "But why didn't she tell him who she really was?"

"She was afraid."

"Afraid? Of what?"

"Afraid Henry would consider her worthless and maybe use her and then toss her aside. She told me she couldn't bear that. She said it would kill her. So long as she was Mrs. Isobel Charles-Greenwood, she knew she was important to him."

"But didn't she realize that Scar would find out sooner or later?"

"She did. But by then Anne hoped she'd have made Henry fall in love with her." Isobel hesitated. "He's already" — she searched for the right word — "used her." The girl drew the collar of Matt's coat higher around her ears. "I told you she's not logical. She's also not very intelligent."

Matt nodded, remembering the painted china doll with the vacant blue eyes. Maybe she was the kind to fall for a vicious outlaw.

Festus brought Isobel tea and the young woman accepted it gratefully. "Marshal," she asked, holding the hot cup gingerly, "what happens next?"

"I don't know what happens next," Matt said, his jaw set hard and unmoving. "I guess we wait."

"For what?" Isobel asked.

"For the dawn," the big marshal answered.

Chapter 26

Sunup Showdown

The sky above Dodge City brightened copper red, streaked by thin bands of violet and jade cloud. The town's storm-battered buildings were touched by pale scarlet light and their long, rectangular shadows lay blue on the fallen snow. From somewhere across the railroad tracks a rooster sang his raucous song to the new day, then fell silent, content to let the racketing echoes of its crowing clamor through the empty streets, falling like tumbling tin cans into the taut quiet.

Matt Dillon was wakened from an uneasy doze and he shook Festus awake. "It's sunup," he whispered.

The deputy blinked like an owl, then rose stiff and weary from the floor and glanced outside. "Nothin' movin' out there, Matthew," he said.

Matt nodded. "Not yet. But they'll come, and maybe real soon."

Isobel Charles-Greenwood lay curled up in her chair sleeping, covered by the marshal's coat. She was a plain girl with not the slightest claim to beauty, except for her thick and luxuriant chestnut brown hair.

Matt smiled to himself. Where was it written that a billionaire's daughter had to be lovely?

He shivered in the freezing morning cold and with a pang of regret dearly wished for his coat back. The coat was warm, heavy tan canvas lined with sheepskin, but shivering or no, he could hardly take it from the girl and leave her in her thin shift.

The marshal shook his head. Hell, couldn't she have put on a coat before she escaped from Henry and saved him all this aggravation?

"Kelley!"

Scar Henry's call, though thinned by distance, was nevertheless loud enough for Matt to hear. He picked up his Winchester and hobbled beside Festus, who was already standing at the blown-out window.

"Kelley! Answer me by God or I'll scatter the woman's brains."

There was a note of agitation and even apprehension in the outlaw's voice and Matt smiled. Doc's plan might be working.

Five minutes ticked past. Nothing moved along Front Street but for the fitful wind that pried into every nook and cranny of the town and gusted cold against the marshal's cheek. Somewhere close by a loose shutter banged constantly, a regularly recurring racket calculated to keep a man's nerves on edge.

"Dillon! Are you there?"

Henry again, yelling loud, the outlaw's frustration growing.

From the direction of the Kelley house, three spaced shots hammered apart the dawn quiet.

"Damn you, Kelley, show yourself!"

Beside him, Matt saw Festus smile. "Right about now I'd say ol' Scar's got hisself a belly full of bedsprings, jes' a-wonderin' what's happenin'."

Matt nodded. "And right about now he's deciding whether or not to leave the mayor's house and come looking."

A silence again descended on Dodge and just before noon Isobel woke.

"What's happening?" she asked, her face pale and frightened.

"As of now, not a whole lot," Matt answered. "Henry did some yelling and shooting earlier, but he's been quiet for hours."

"Maybe he's gone," Isobel said, her eyes bright with hope.

The marshal shook his head. "He's around, and pretty soon he's going to come looking for us."

Outside the morning was slowly giving way to a gray afternoon. The sun had risen in the sky, but it was wafer thin and without warmth, the surrounding sky a washed-out blue, like faded denim.

As Matt watched, a hawk glided over the rooftops of the town, then soared a hundred feet higher before folding its wings and plunging like a thrown lance to earth. Somewhere, just beyond the limits of Dodge, a small death had occurred, noticed only by the marshal and the uncaring wind.

Just after one o'clock, by Matt's watch, Henry and Waters appeared on Front Street.

The two outlaws walked with Anne Purdy between them, Henry's gun pressed into the small of the girl's back. Isobel had said Anne Purdy was an actress, but the fear in her china doll eyes was real enough and her small, heart-shaped mouth trembled.

Festus crouched down by the low wall under the ruined saloon window while Matt stood, alert and ready, his Winchester hanging in his right hand.

Henry and Waters stepped along the

boardwalk, always careful to keep Anne in the path of any gunfire. The heads of the two outlaws constantly swiveled this way and that on their shoulders, like men being stalked by a tiger.

One by one, Henry and Waters checked out the banks in town, Henry's face growing blacker with rage every time he swung back into the line of Matt's sight.

The outlaws stepped back along the boardwalk and stopped opposite the Long Branch. Watching through a small hole in the wall, Matt saw Henry's slow gaze sweep speculatively across the ruined building. He turned and said something to Waters, but the gunman shook his head and said something in return — urgent words, Matt judged.

Henry stood in silence for a few moments, deep in thought, then nodded, agreeing with whatever Waters had said.

The gunman hitched his gun belt higher on his hips, then walked away from Henry, in the direction of the Kelley house. Henry turned and, keeping the girl close to him, headed toward the livery stable.

Matt ignored Henry, his eyes fixed on Waters.

Slowly, he lifted the Winchester to his shoulder and sighted on the nape of Waters' neck, just under the gunman's hat. The big lawman moved the sights lower, until they were square and steady between Waters' shoulder blades. He held his breath and took up the slack on the trigger.

All he had to do was squeeze and Waters would be dead, his spine smashed by the impact of the big .44.40 bullet.

Despite the cold, sweat beaded Matt's forehead and his mouth was dry. Waters was now thirty yards away, walking slowly, his spurs ringing in the quiet.

All he had to do was squeeze. . . .

The skin of his face suddenly tight, Matt lowered the rifle.

He couldn't do it. He couldn't shoot a man in the back, not even a low-life killer like Deacon Waters.

He had to abide by his code.

Years before, a few men who lived by the gun had tried to convince Matt that his way was wrong and that their way of getting the drop on a man was the right and only way.

One of those men was John Wesley Hardin. "Matt, getting the drop don't mean drawing down on a man to see who's faster," Wes had told him. "There's too many fast men out there and it's a surefire way to lose your scalp. No, you kill a man any way you can, while he's kneeling at his prayers, while he's in bed asleep with his wife, when you catch him without a gun or he's got his back turned to you or he's a-bouncing his bonny baby boy on his knee."

Hardin had tested his whiskey and looked at Matt over the rim of the glass, his blue eyes shot through with ice. "And any time you can, bushwhack him and cut him in half with a shotgun." The gunman had nodded, agreeing with his own raw-boned wisdom. "Young feller, that's what they mean by getting the drop on a man, and never you forget it."

Well, that was Wes Hardin's way, but it had never been Matt Dillon's.

He'd grown to manhood in a hard land surrounded by hard men, and a couple of them had introduced him to a philosophy far removed from Hardin's, the principle that you met a man while he was belted and ready, and facing you.

It was a more dangerous way, the code of the gunfighter, but it helped a man sleep nights and kept his conscience clean.

"I wondered if you'd pull that trigger," Festus said, lifting his eyes to Matt from his place at the window.

"I came close," Matt said.

"No, you didn't, Matthew," Festus said.

"You wasn't close a-tall."

"What would you have done?" the marshal asked.

"Pulled the trigger. Maybe I would, if'n I was scared enough."

A smile touched Matt's lips. "I'm plenty scared enough. Later I could regret it."

Festus' eyes slanted to the street again and he shrugged, his brow knotted in thought. But he said nothing further.

Matt Dillon now faced a choice. Should he go after Henry or Waters?

He thought it through for a few moments, then made his decision. Without Henry, Waters would be cut adrift and lack direction. Matt knew his first duty was to ensure the safety of Dodge, and from that point of view, Henry was the more dangerous man.

It would be Henry then — and later Waters.

"If Waters makes to come back this way, hold him off with your rifle as long as you can," Matt told Festus.

The deputy nodded. "Sure will, Matthew."

Matt's eyes angled down to his fellow lawman. "Don't play the hero, Festus. If Waters gets too close, fog it out of here and find a place to hole up." He turned to

Isobel. "And keep her out of the line of fire."

"Goin' after Henry, huh?" Festus asked.

"I think it's time, don't you?"

"Maybe so," the deputy said, conflicting emotions bunched up in his pale, strained face. "Step careful, Matthew." He hesitated a few heartbeats. "An' good luck."

Matt nodded, touched the brim of his hat with the barrel of his Winchester, then thumped on his crutch to the back of the saloon. He planned on taking the long way around to the livery stable, where he'd be less likely to be spotted by Deacon Waters.

Stepping tentatively through the fallen snow, now crusted with ice that crunched under his feet, the marshal left the Long Branch, then made his way past the rear of several other buildings that fronted the street.

The day had brightened but the temperature was still below zero and Matt's open mouth steamed gray as he labored through the deeper drifts. A driving wind, cold as a stepmother's breath, blew off the plains and the marshal shivered. He had no coat and was dressed only in tan canvas pants, blue wool shirt and leather vest. His left foot, inadequately protected by its thin sock, was numb and his broken leg pained him considerably.

He knew he was in no shape to face a skilled gunman like Scar Henry, a thought that brought him much unease and did little to add to his confidence. As far as was possible, he kept working the fingers of his gun hand, fearing they'd stiffen into a frozen claw around the icy steel action of the Winchester.

Slowly, taking care, Matt plodded alongside Darcy Green's Dress Shop, then crossed Front Street. He was in the street, wide-open, for almost a full minute, but to his relief, by the time he reached the opposite boardwalk, he'd seen no sign of Waters.

His crutch thumping on ice-slicked pine, Matt made his way along the boardwalk, then stepped down and crossed the twenty yards of open ground that brought him to the livery stable.

The marshal had just reached the barn when Henry stepped outside, his left arm around Anne Purdy's waist, his Colt holstered on his right hip.

Henry's eyebrows shot up in surprise. Then slowly a vicious, triumphant grin stole across his thin mouth. "Well, if'n it ain't Matt Dillon," he said. His eyes held on Matt, devoid of any trace of humanity or feeling. Henry's lips were parted, his teeth with their long, pointed canines gleaming with saliva. He was breathing just a little bit hard, not from exertion but from the excitement of the approaching kill. There was a bloodstained rent on the left shoulder of his mackinaw, where Matt's bullet had burned him, and the outlaw's face had a look of reptilian evil in the raw afternoon light, the scar on his cheek a terrible thing.

Involuntarily, Matt took a step back.

"Where the hell is everybody, lawman?" Henry asked, his quick black eyes noticing the big marshal's uneasy movement.

Matt found his voice and was pleased that his words were firm, without a trace of tremble. "They've all gone, Scar. Gone to a place where you won't find them."

"The money from the banks with them? And the horses?"

The marshal nodded and smiled. "You've lost, Scar. You can't leave Dodge and before long the cavalry will be here. Of course, if you're lucky, you might starve to death. There isn't a scrap of food left in the whole town."

Henry's tongue touched his upper lip. Then he grabbed Anne Purdy by the arm and dragged her in front of him. "You're wrong. I still got my bargaining chip. I got her."

Matt shook his head. "You got nothing, Scar. That isn't Isobel" — he searched his memory for the name — "Charles-Greenwood. The woman you have there is an out-of-work actress by the name of Anne Purdy. The real heiress was the little, skinny maid, Scar, and I've got her safe."

"The maid?" Henry asked, confusion balling up in his face.

"That's right, the maid. It seems her rich daddy was worried she would get kidnapped way out here in the Wild West, so he paid the woman you have there to take her place." Matt waited a few moments, then added: "So you see, Scar, you have nothing."

"You're lying, Dillon," Henry growled. "You're trying to protect the woman."

Matt shook his head. "Would I lie to you now things are going so bad for you?"

Henry wrenched Anne Purdy around to face him, and the girl let out a little gasp of pain and fear as he shook her. "Is this true? Is what he's saying true?"

"I love you, Dave," Anne sobbed.

"Damn you, is it true?"

The girl nodded, her blue eyes red with tears. "Yes, it's true." Her voice rose to a frantic level. "But it doesn't make any difference. I still love you. Take me with you, Dave. Let's leave this place. I'll go anywhere you want."

Anger was black on Henry's face as he swung on Matt. "Bring the real heiress here — now. Or by God Dillon, I'll shoot this woman."

Matt's smile was thin. "Then shoot away, Scar. She doesn't mean a thing to me."

"No!" Anne cried, her fingers opening and closing. "I love you, Dave. I want to marry you."

"Me marry you?" Henry asked in mock surprise, his mouth a tight angry gash. "You've already given me everything I wanted from you and I don't need you anymore. Hell, I don't marry whores. I use them hard, then toss them away like garbage."

"Please don't say that, Dave," Ann howled. "You know you love me. Tell me you do."

"You cheap whore," Henry snarled. "How could I love a stupid alley cat like you? You're nothing. Less than nothing."

The girl looked up at Henry and read something vile in his eyes. She screamed like someone in terrible pain. Her hand, fingers curled like talons, shot up and her long nails raked from the scar on Henry's cheek to his chin, digging deep, drawing four sudden streaks of blood.

The gunman roared and drew his Colt. He pushed the woman away from him and leveled the gun at her belly.

"Scar!" Matt yelled. He levered a round into the Winchester.

Henry turned, his eyes ablaze, his Colt swinging fast on the marshal.

Shooting from the hip, Matt fired, cranked another round into the chamber and fired again.

Hit twice, Henry stumbled back. The outlaw fired and Matt felt the bullet tug at his hat. The marshal racked the Winchester again, an ejected brass cartridge case glinting in the weak sunlight, and hammered a third round into Henry's chest.

The outlaw slammed against the stable wall, and his gun slipped from suddenly weak fingers. Henry stayed there for a few moments, then shot his arm straight out, his finger pointed at Matt.

"Yoooooou!" he roared, a primal bellow that erupted from the open cavern of his mouth. Henry's eyes were fixed on Matt, red rimmed, the scarlet talon furrows on his cheek running blood. The outlaw took a single step toward Matt, his accusing finger still spiking at the lawman's face. Another staggering step, one more, and then his eyes darkened, and like a great felled oak, he dropped flat on his face, all the life suddenly leaving him.

Anne Purdy cried out and dropped to her knees beside the fallen outlaw, the right side of her face pressed to his back. "Dave," she whimpered, "tell me you're not dead! Tell me you love me, Dave. Tell me! Tell me!"

Feeling slightly sick, Matt turned away in time to see Mayor Kelley loping along Front Street on Buck, several other horsemen strung out behind him.

The mayor pulled up the bay in a flurry of snow and jumped from the saddle.

"Matt, are you all right?" he asked.

The marshal nodded. "So far," he said, propping the butt of his rifle against his hip, his hand on the stock.

Kelley nodded to the dead man in the snow. "Henry?"

"He was," Matt answered. A slight smile touched his lips. "I always figured a Winchester was better than a Henry."

Chapter 27

Vanishing Act

"There's no sign of him? You've looked everywhere?"

"Everywhere, Mr. Kelley," Newly O'Brien answered, his face bleak. "It's like he's vanished off the face of the earth."

Matt nodded from his chair by his desk. "You tried, Newly. But I've got a feeling Waters will show up sooner or later." He turned to Kelley. "How come you arrived when you did, Mayor?"

The little Irishman shrugged. "We got to talking about it after we reached the train, Matt," he said. "It didn't set right with us leaving you here, so we headed back." Kelley's face was lumpy with disappointment. "Too late, it seems."

Matt let that go and asked: "When are the others returning?"

The mayor shrugged. "Probably tomorrow morning. By that time they'll have burned the last of the firewood."

"How is Lieutenant Greenwood?"

"Doc says he'll live."

"His wife is eager to be reacquainted."

Matt's eyes slid to the window, where Percy Crump was leading a melancholy procession, behind him the frozen bodies of the dead cavalrymen jolting along in an open wagon.

Kelley saw it too, and his anger flared. "Damn it all, Matt! A man just doesn't disappear. Waters has got to be around Dodge somewhere."

"I'll find him, Mayor," Matt said. "Or he'll find me."

Kelley let that go and changed the subject. "How is Festus?"

"He's in bed." Matt smiled. "And eagerly awaiting the return of the adoring ladies of Dodge."

"That's where you should be too, Marshal. In bed."

"Not so long as Waters is on the loose."

Kelley stepped to the window and glanced outside. "Kitty is over there talking to John Carter. It looks like she's lining up him and his five sons to rebuild her saloon."

"Mrs. Isobel What's-her-name says her daddy will pay for it," Matt said. "And maybe he will."

"A fine girl, Mrs. Charles-Greenwood," Kelley said. "Not as pretty as the other one, but a lot more pleasant. She told me she'll be sure to mention to her father that I was instrumental in saving her life. Oh, and she asked my wife if she had the makings to bake another apple-and-raisin pie." The mayor nodded to himself, beaming. "Yes, a very fine girl indeed."

Outside the afternoon was shading into night. The air was cold and smelled of snow, and since none of the lamps were lit along Front Street, shadows were creeping stealthily into the alleys. In the distance the coyotes talked and the wind carried their calls to Dodge, spreading the high-pitched yaps around town like idle gossip.

For the fourth or fifth time that day, Matt slid his Colt out of the holster and spun the cylinder to check the loads. He thumbed back the hammer and eased it down on an empty chamber before sliding the gun back into its oiled leather scabbard.

Kelley had turned and he'd been watching. "You won't be alone, you know," he said, his eyes aglow. "Me and a few others will stand at your side."

Matt nodded. "Thanks, Mayor, but it won't happen that way. Waters will come after me and we'll meet at a time and place of his choosing. Believe me, neither you nor anyone else will be around."

"We'll see about that," Kelley snapped. "I'm not letting you out of my sight until that killer is flushed out of hiding and arrested or shot." Kelley waited a few moments until the blood left his burning cheeks, then said in a kinder tone: "Anyhow, Marshal, now I study on it, you'll be spending the next few weeks in bed until that leg heals. Me and the rest of the citizens of Dodge will deal with Deacon Waters."

Matt saw no point in arguing. Kelley didn't understand what drove Waters. Like the rich sportsmen who traveled to Africa to shoot big game, he was a trophy hunter. There would be little credit in putting the head of a bumbling city mayor on his wall. But to Waters, the head of Matt Dillon, a named man, was a very different proposition.

Kitty stepped into the marshal's office just as full darkness descended on Dodge. She wore a dark blue coat that fell just short of the floor, revealing slim ankles in polished high-button boots, and her unbound hair lay over her shoulders, shining like molten gold.

"Kelley said you were talking to John Carter," Matt said, his heart thumping in his chest at the sight of her.

Kitty nodded. "He says he'll have it finished well before the herds arrive. Isobel Charles-Greenwood told me she'll ask her father to foot the bill."

"Heard that," Matt acknowledged.

Kitty sat on the edge of Matt's desk and for a few moments she said nothing. She touched a place on her cheek, then asked finally: "Any sign of Waters?"

Matt shook his head.

"Maybe he's gone," Kitty said.

"Gone where? There's nowhere for him to go, unless he can find a horse. The mayor has posted guards at all the livery stables and barns in town, so it won't be easy for him."

"Matt," Kitty said, a pleading urgency in her eyes, "maybe you should leave. The mayor has this thing well in hand. He can do without your help for a few weeks. By the time you come back, Waters will be gone — or dead."

The marshal was silent, as though deep in thought. After a while he said: "Deacon Waters shot my crutch out from under me."

"What's that got to do with you leaving?" Kitty asked.

"Everything," Matt answered. "I landed

in the dirt of the barn floor, horse dung and straw in my hair, and lay there like a helpless cripple while he stood over me, grinning. A man doesn't forget a thing like that. At least this man doesn't."

"Pride," Kitty said, blood pooling scarlet on her cheeks. "It's just mindless, masculine pride."

Matt nodded. "Could be. Maybe it is."

Kitty reached out and laid her fingers on the back of the big lawman's hand. "Matt, saddle up Buck. Take me with you. I'll go anywhere you want — just name the place."

"Any other time I'd jump at that chance, Kitty," Matt laughed. "But not now, not with this thing hanging over me."

Kitty's fingers slid away from Matt's hand and she stood, her back stiff, her lovely face enameled with frustrated anger.

"Don't expect me to be there, Matt," she said, her voice trembling.

"Where?" Matt asked, taken aback.

"At your funeral," Kitty said.

She stomped across the floor, threw open the door and stepped into darkness.

Two hours after first light the following morning, the people returned to Dodge.

Lieutenant Greenwood looked pale and

gaunt but seemed to be improving under Doc Adams's care.

"That young man is mighty anxious to see his wife," Doc told Matt. "Where is she?"

"At the mayor's house," Matt answered. "She's there with Anne Purdy. Trying to console her, I guess."

"What happened, Matt?" Doc asked, reading the strain in the marshal's face.

Matt told Doc about finding Isobel in an alley and his gunfight with Scar Henry.

"Waters escaped," he said, summing it up. "And I've no idea where he is."

Doc's brow wrinkled in concern. "That's bad news, Matt," he said. "Waters is a killer and he's dangerous."

"Tell me something I don't already know, Doc," the marshal said. He paused for a moment, then added: "Mayor Kelley says he'll hunt him down."

"Will he?"

"I doubt it," Matt answered, "not unless Waters wants to be found."

Shortly after noon, a full troop of Buffalo Soldier cavalry led by an elderly gray-haired captain named Canfield rode into Dodge.

Matt had to recount how Greenwood was wounded and his troopers killed. "All but one," the marshal said, his face grim, "and I reckon he's still running."

Canfield shook his head. "No, he's back at the fort, but the man is so shaken I think his soldiering days may be over." The captain's faded gray eyes lifted to Matt's face. "A bad business, Marshal. And you say this man Waters has disappeared?"

"Seems like," Matt answered. "At least we haven't been able to find him so far."

"If you don't mind, I'll have my men search," Canfield said. "We'll turn over this town until we find him."

"Suits me, Captain," Matt said. "But don't let your men go anywhere alone. Deacon Waters is good with a gun and he's deadly."

"Sound advice, Marshal," Canfield said. He touched his hat with three fingers. "Now, if you will excuse me, I will go deploy my troop."

Three hours later the captain returned to Matt's office, his shoulders slumped in defeat. "We searched everywhere, but couldn't find hide nor hair of Waters," Canfield said. "And I mean everywhere. I even took a pass through the house of some poor crazy woman across the tracks."

"Her name is Jane Morgan," Matt said.

"Her husband was killed by Henry and Waters."

The captain shook his head, turning dejected eyes to Matt. "I must confess, I'm at a loss, Marshal. I just don't know what else I can do. I've already told Mrs. Charles-Greenwood that I'm ready to escort her back to the fort."

"Take Lieutenant Greenwood and his wife to Fort Dodge, Captain. If Waters shows up, I'll handle him."

As Greenwood had done earlier, Canfield's dubious gaze took in Matt's crutch and the ragged splints on his leg. "I can leave you some men," he said. "Say a dozen troopers under the command of my sergeant. He's a first-class soldier, Sergeant Hill. If Waters shows up, he'll know how to deal with him."

"I appreciate the offer, Captain," Matt said. "I'm sure Mayor Kelley will find quarters for your men."

Before Canfield could reply, the door opened and Isobel stepped inside. She was dressed in a warm cloak and she carried Matt's coat over her arm.

"I would just like to return this, Marshal, and thank you for all you've done," she said. "You saved my life when you found me in the alley."

Matt smiled. "Glad I was around." He took his coat from the girl and hung it on a hook beside the gun rack. "When are you leaving for the fort?"

"As soon as Captain Canfield gives the order."

The soldier glanced at the clock on the wall. "Right after I talk to the mayor," he said. "And that's something I plan on doing now." Canfield extended his hand to Matt. "Good luck, Marshal. And please feel free to call on my men."

Matt shook the soldier's hand. Then the captain bowed to Isobel and left.

"I must be going too," Isobel said. She smiled her plain smile. "It seems my husband doesn't want me out of his sight for a minute."

"Where is Anne Purdy?" the marshal asked.

"I gave her some money," Isobel said. "She plans to stay at the Dodge House, then catch a train east just as soon as the weather breaks." The girl's eyes clouded. "She really is a poor thing. She just fell in love with the wrong man was all."

Matt nodded. "Yup, I'd sure say so." His eyes went to the girl's face. "Then so long, Mrs. . . . um . . ."

"Isobel is just fine, Marshal," the girl

said, her smile widening.

"Isobel it is," Matt said. He reached down and took the woman's hand in his. "So long, Isobel, and take good care of your wounded soldier boy."

After the woman was gone, Matt sat at his desk, the cup of coffee in front of him slowly growing cold. He also knew he should be hungry but he had little appetite for food.

Deacon Waters was too much on his mind.

Where was he?

Somehow he had to find him.

Chapter 28

Swan Song of a Gunman

"Cold morning, Matt." Doc Adams unbuttoned his coat, shook out a few stray snowflakes, then perched on the corner of Matt's desk. "And by the way," the physician added, "you look like hell."

The big marshal smiled. "Thanks, Doc. Have you any more good news?"

"Just this, you should be in bed resting that leg. I swear, if you walk around on it much longer, it's never going to heal."

"After I find Deacon Waters," Matt said.

Doc shook his head, irritation sharp in his eyes. "Waters is long gone. If a whole troop of cavalry couldn't find him, he's no longer in Dodge City."

"He's here, Doc. I can feel his presence. It's like the smell of death that wraps around him is being carried in the wind."

"Matt," Doc grumbled, ignoring what the lawman had just said, "as your doctor I'm ordering you to bed. For at least three weeks. And if need be I'll call in Kitty to help me get you there."

A smile tugged at the corners of Matt's mouth. "I don't think Kitty will help. She's not too happy with me at the moment."

"That's because she's worried about you, for God's sake. She told me all about how you intend to go after Waters. My advice to you is to forget about it. Waters isn't here. After you killed Henry, he lit out to save his own skin."

"He's here, Doc. Like I told you, I can smell him."

Doc rose and loudly clapped his hands together in exasperation. "That's it. I'm out of here. I'll send Kitty over and see if she can talk some sense into you."

"How come you're up and about so early, Doc?" Matt said, changing the subject. "You don't normally open your surgery until nine."

Doc's face was suddenly bleak, a tangle of emotion in his eyes. "I went to visit that Jane Morgan woman." He shook his head. "I can't do anything for her."

"I wonder if she knows that I killed the man who murdered her husband?" Matt asked, more to himself than to Doc.

But the physician answered. "I don't think she knows anything," he said. "I don't think she even knows she's in this world. Her mind has gone to a dark place I can't reach. Modern medicine has its limitations, and I reckon I've just discovered mine."

"Think I should try and talk to her?" Matt asked. "Tell her about Henry?"

Doc shrugged. "It can't do any harm, and it might do some good." He hesitated a moment or two, then added: "Sure, why not? Talk to her. And afterward, get off that leg and into bed." Doc stomped to the door, stopped and threw over his shoulder: "And that's an order, Marshal Dillon."

After Doc left, Matt thought about Jane Morgan sitting in her dark house, a prisoner of her own grief and growing madness. Could he help her? Doc said it was worth a try.

The big marshal made up his mind. He rose, found his crutch and struggled into his coat. He took a step toward the door, turned and picked up the coffee from his desk. It was only lukewarm, but he drained the cup, set it down, then walked out onto the boardwalk.

The morning was bright. The temperature had risen and beads of melted ice fell steadily from the icicles hanging along the buildings on Front Street. Now that Dodge had come back to life, the snow had turned to slush, churned up in the street by horses and wagons to the color of tobacco juice. The sky was pale blue, touched by gold to the east, with a few slender strands of violet cloud at the horizon.

Matt crossed the tracks and made his slow way to Jane Morgan's house, finding slush every bit as treacherous and unpredictable as snow. As he struggled closer he saw that all the windows were open, no doubt at the insistence of Martha Owens, allowing light and fresh air to enter Jane Morgan's dark world.

The big marshal opened the front gate and stepped onto the path leading to the front door when a man, leading a buckskin horse with an Army saddle, stepped around the corner.

It was Deacon Waters.

"Saw you coming a ways, Matt," the gunman said. "Figured I'd just wait. Saved me coming to look for you."

Waters had let go of the buckskin's reins, and his hands were close to the Smith & Wesson Russians on his thighs. The man's blue eyes were calm and untroubled, but glinted with an icy light. They were the eyes of a man who knew he would soon kill.

Matt played for time. Somebody — Sergeant Hill and his soldiers maybe — might ride this way. "Where have you been hiding, Waters?" he asked. "Here?"

The gunman shook his head. "In the last place anyone would look, among the stacked dead at Percy Crump's place. Hell, no one wanted to go in there, and when they did, they sure didn't look around." A smile touched Waters' thin mouth. "Ol' Scar was lying there. Looked all peaceful, just like he was sleeping. Of course, he had three of your bullets in him. Messed him up some."

"I guess you were right at home there, Waters, in a place of the dead."

The man shrugged. "It was quiet. Cold though, but mighty peaceful." Waters' mouth hardened into a thin line. "I got to be on my way, Matt." He jerked his head in the direction of the buckskin. "Pretty soon they'll find the dead soldier boy who rode that."

The gunman's eyes iced over like ponds in winter. "I told you once that I'd end it before I left and . . . well . . . like I said, I'm leaving." The gunman smiled. "No hard feelings?"

His hands flashed for his guns.

Even as he drew, Matt knew he was way too slow. Waters' guns were out and leveling and he still hadn't cleared leather.

A shot blasted the morning apart.

Waters, hit hard, staggered back, scarlet blossoming on the front of his shirt. He looked at Matt in stunned horror, wondering how he could have been hit.

Another shot hammered into the silence, and Waters was hit again, higher this time, just where his neck met the top of his chest.

The gunman stopped where he was and his eyes slid to his left. "No!" he screamed. "Not you!"

Jane Morgan stood at the open window, her face stark white, a smoking Winchester in her hands. Her husband's hunting rifle.

Waters spun on weakening legs, his guns coming up, all his hatred and despair now fixed on the woman.

Matt and Jane Morgan fired at the same time.

Two bullets crashed into Waters' chest and the gunman went down, slamming into the front legs of his horse. The buckskin whinnied in fear and backed away, kicking out with its hooves, and Waters was thrown onto his back.

His Colt ready, Matt stepped to the fallen man and looked down at him. Waters' face was a frozen mask of horror. "It wasn't supposed to be like this," he gasped, blood bubbling over his bottom lip. "Not like this."

Matt nodded. "Yeah, things are tough all over."

But Waters didn't hear. Matt Dillon was talking to a dead man.

Behind him the marshal heard a door open and turned as Jane Morgan stepped onto the porch, Martha Owens, looking pale with fright, close behind her.

"Is he dead?" Jane asked, her voice flat, emotionless.

Matt nodded, saying nothing.

"And the other one?"

"I done for him," Matt said.

"Then it's over?" Jane asked. "My husband can finally rest in peace?"

"It's over, Mrs. Morgan," Matt said. "It's all over."

The woman let go of the Winchester and the rifle clattered to the ground at her feet. She buried her face in her hands and began to sob violently, all the tightly knotted emotions wrenching out of her.

Martha Owens put a plump, motherly arm around Jane's shoulders. "That's it, dear," she soothed. "Let it out, let it all out. You'll feel better."

She led Jane Morgan into the house and

quietly closed the door behind her.

Matt turned and saw soldiers led by a sergeant running toward him. Close on their heels were dozens of townspeople led by a red-faced Mayor Kelley. Kitty was among them.

Chapter 29

Heroes and Calico Cats

Matt Dillon lay in his bed at the Dodge House, Doc Adams and Mayor Kelley standing on either side of him.

"You did a fine job, Matt." Kelley beamed. "You saved this town and that's something I'll never forget."

"No, Mayor, it wasn't me, and it wasn't Festus who saved Dodge," Matt said. "It was the very thing both Henry and Waters despised most — women."

Kelley's eyebrows rose in surprise. "Women? How do you figure that?"

"Henry believed women were made to be used and abused, and then tossed away like an empty peach can," Matt explained. "Waters considered women worthless, all of them whores. But in the end, it was the women they held in such contempt who killed them.

"Kitty started it by allowing the Long Branch to be sacrificed. Then Anne Purdy used her nails on Henry, distracting him long enough for me to gun him. And in the end, it wasn't me who done for Deacon Waters, probably the fastest, deadliest gunman who ever lived. It was Jane Morgan."

Matt smiled. "Never underestimate the power of a woman, Mayor. It was petticoats, not pistols, that saved Dodge."

"And speaking of the power of women, Kitty is waiting outside the door," Doc said. He turned to Kelley and raised an eyebrow. "Perhaps this would be an opportune time to make our exit, Mayor?"

Kelley nodded, his eyes lowering to Matt. "I'd like to continue this discussion some other time, Matt," he said. "There's no more powerful woman than Mrs. Kelley, I assure you. I'd like to hear your opinion on her."

Matt smiled and waved a hand. "Anytime, Mayor. I'm becoming a real expert on the fairer sex."

"You just don't understand women, Matt," Kitty said. "We often say things we don't mean. All that stuff about not coming to your funeral — that was just empty talk."

"Glad to hear it, Kitty." Matt smiled. "Not that I've any intention of dying anytime soon."

Kitty placed a carpetbag on the floor, its

sides now and then bulging as something moved inside. "Matt, I have to leave to supervise John Carter. He wants to get started rebuilding the Long Branch right away. She smiled and bent down toward the squirming bag. "I'll be right back, but in the meantime I've brought you a little friend to keep you company while you're confined to bed for the next three weeks."

Kitty opened the bag and released a ragged, outraged calico cat. "Isn't she cute?" she asked. "I found her wandering near the hotel. You two were just made for each other."

"But, Kitty —" Matt began.

"No buts, Matt. You'll need a little companion while you're lying in bed all by yourself." Kitty walked to the door. "See you real soon."

As soon as Kitty was gone, the calico jumped up on the bed, studied the lay of the land for a few moments, then settled herself on top of Matt's broken leg, her baleful green eyes fixed on the marshal's.

Matt knew this cat. He knew her from way back.

He'd had run-ins with the animal before, usually over the right of way on the boardwalk — a series of tense, ill-humored confrontations he'd invariably lost. For some reason the calico bore a grudge against him and was always on the prod.

Through the thin wall separating his room from the one next door, Matt heard the high-pitched giggles of the fashionable Dodge City belles as they pampered and fussed over Festus, their wounded hero.

The calico continued to stare at him belligerently, remembering a dozen desperate encounters past, forgiving none of them.

Matt's head slammed into his pillow as the cat glared and the giggles next door grew louder.

He groaned and held his head in his hands.

It was going to be a long three weeks.

About the Author

As a little boy growing up in a small fishing village in Scotland, ***Joseph A. West*** enjoyed many happy Saturday mornings at the local cinema in the company of Roy and Gene and Hoppy. His lifelong ambition was to become a cowboy, but he was sidetracked by a career in law enforcement and journalism. He now resides with his wife and daughter in Palm Beach, Florida, where he enjoys horse riding, cowboy action shooting, and studying Western history.

The employees of Thorndike Press hope you have enjoyed this Large Print book. All our Thorndike and Wheeler Large Print titles are designed for easy reading, and all our books are made to last. Other Thorndike Press Large Print books are available at your library, through selected bookstores, or directly from us.

For information about titles, please call:

(800) 223-1244

or visit our Web site at:

www.gale.com/thorndike
www.gale.com/wheeler

To share your comments, please write:

Publisher
Thorndike Press
295 Kennedy Memorial Drive
Waterville, ME 04901